Mrs. N. Furlong

Cozenza, a Tale of Italy, and other Poems

Mrs. N. Furlong

Cozenza, a Tale of Italy, and other Poems

ISBN/EAN: 9783743305076

Manufactured in Europe, USA, Canada, Australia, Japa

Cover: Foto ©Andreas Hilbeck / pixelio.de

Manufactured and distributed by brebook publishing software
(www.brebook.com)

Mrs. N. Furlong

Cozenza, a Tale of Italy, and other Poems

Mrs N. Furlong.

COZENZA,

A TALE OF ITALY,

AND

OTHER POEMS.

———

BY MRS. N. FURLONG.

———

ILLUSTRATED EDITION.

SAN FRANCISCO:
PRINTED BY B. F. STERETT, 532 CLAY STREET.
1880.

INDEX.

	PAGE.
PREFACE.	13
ANNOUNCEMENT	14
INVOCATION	17
COZENZA, A TALE OF ITALY	19
NONNENWERTH, A LEGEND OF THE RHINE	133
WHERE SHE SLEEPS IN SANTA CLARA	225
ET ELLE EST MUETTE.	226
REMEMBRANCE	227
AN ANSWER	228
LAMENT OF LEONORA D'ESTE	229
STAR OF THE SEA.	242
ALTSAY BURN	243
TORTESA AND MURILLO.	250
SISTER MARY AGNES	252
A PHILOSOPHIC ASSURANCE	254
THE "BEER SWILL"	255

ILLUSTRATIONS.

PORTRAIT OF THE AUTHOR.

CASTLE OF OLEVANO.	THE LURLY.
ARCH OF ROLANDSECK.	CONVENT OF NONNENWERTH.
THE BRIDGE ACROSS THE NAHE.	ALTSAY BURN.

PREFACE.

On account of the advertisements to the two larger poems which constitute nearly the whole of this book,—together with the numerous notes attached, explaining so much of the subject, there is little left to be said by way of preface,—except to thank the public, and a numerous list of subscribing friends, for the favorable acceptance and criticism accorded the first edition of " Nounenwerth," and to hope that in the Poem of "Cozenza," an equally desired praise and sustaining influence may be deserved, and accorded. It has become, perhaps, too much the custom of authors to seem to depreciate their own efforts; I will only say that I have not tried to "send forth a leaf floating," or "a straw on the wind," or any thing of that kind. I have earnestly tried to please my dear readers, and hope they will think so.

Mrs. N. Furlong.

·ANNOUNCEMENT.

———

This Poem is partly founded on the story of a Revolutionary Sicilian. Some of the Characters are real—others fictitious. Cozenza, the principal character, becomes the leader of Revolutionists, in obedience to the wish of his father, who suffered death at the hands of the reigning Monarch. Imbued with the patriotism of his sire, he makes heroic efforts to achieve the Liberation of Italy. While engaged in battle, he is wounded, taken prisoner, and confined in *Castell á Mare*. He effects his escape, but dies while trying to reach the mountains.

Etolia, a young lady of noble family, a daughter of the count of Olevano, is made the wife of Cozenza after many romantic trials. At the beginning of the Revolution, she retires to her home at Olevano. Suspected of treason, she is thrown into the dungeons of her own Castle, by the secret spies of the King: and, refusing to confess the complicity of her husband in the Revolution, is put to death, by torture, expiring in the hands of her persecutors.

Salluzzi, a Captain of Bandits, compelled Cardinal Capano, whom he had taken captive, to unite in marriage Cozenza and Etolia in the Robber's cave where Cozenza had accidentally met his betrothed. Salluzzi renounces his reckless life, and, with his band joins the Liberators. Concetta Lavagna, the wife of one of Salluzzi's men, seeks her husband on the field of battle among the slain, but finds Cozenza, in the arms of death, and receives his last words of hope and despair. Caldara, a patriot priest, while alleviating the poor, gives his service to the cause of Liberty.

Morbili, Pontillo, Del Carretto, Satriano, Maniscalco, and others, are secret spies of the King; and, by machines of torture exact confession from those suspected of being disloyal.

Localities, and Historic events pertaining to the Revolution of 1848, are carefully detailed from authentic sources.

A TALE OF ITALY.

A POEM IN EIGHT CANTOS.

INVOCATION.

Once more, sweet Muse, inspire my soul
To wake the Harp, its chords control,
   And pleasing verse unfold;
Lend me the voice to fill my song
With strains as pure, if not so strong,
   As bards have sung of old.

Let fitting thought, in verse arise;
Of classic lands, neath sunny skies,
   Made sacred by the lore,
Which grand poetic minds have cast
Upon the record of the past,
   Of fair Italia's shore.

Then swell the heart to feel the strain
Of simple music, which has lain
   Cold in the breast so long;
And may the task of love be mine,
Thy tender laurels to entwine,
   To beautify my song.

COZENZA.

A TALE OF ITALY.

CANTO FIRST.

I.

FROM sweet Palermo's fruited vales,
　To Genoa's white moving sails;
Ravine and oak, and walnut shade,
And clust'ring vine in sylvan glade,
And quaint, receding peasant cots,
That rise like wings from hillside grots—
Are scenes that claim the gifted hand
Of magic thought; for, scenes more grand,
From mountain slope to ocean strand,—
Seek not beyond this classic land.
Here, blood of murdered Cæsars flowed;—
Here, Carthagenian troopers rode
O'er roadways where proud armies vast
Swept by with death and blighting blast,
And left defeat to mark the past.
The trampling hoofs of Hannibal,

No passing sounds to-day recall;
And wintry floods, a thousand times,
Have washed the crimson fields of crimes.
Here, ruins drenching in the flood
Of ages, now not stained with blood
Of tyrants; and the wild winds brood
In sadness where some fortress stood—
The tyrant hand, the martyred faith,
Alike, devoted spoils of Death.

II.

Coliseum, crumbling to decay!
What shall I say that is not said:—
Thy multitudes have passed away.
Thy bleeding martyr, and the gray
Fierce panther that upon him fed;
And thy arena to the night
And day is domeless, roofless, quite:
And where the busy surging throng
Of cities waked the morn, the song
Of shepherd swain is heard among
His flocks, as though the restless tongue
Of fame, with silver harp unstrung,
Had left her noblest songs, unsung.
Where now, the arm of valor tried?
Where now, the ancient halls of pride?
Let ruin tell—the only guide.

III.

At Cannae, whose historic plain ,
Saw forty thousand Romans slain
By foreign foe, no signs remain

Of former greatness; and in vain,
We seek the dirty lanes of noise,
Old dames, and ragged beggar boys
So idly dreaming time away—
Its memory scarcely lives to-day.

IV.

Along Voltorno's vale, the rain[2]
And sun, still fresh the growing grain,
And ever toiling sleepless bees,
Go laden on in droning hum;
And birds of song, at morning come
And thrill the fruited orange trees.

V.

Gaeta only lives in name;[3]
And were it not for Virgil fame,
A passing notice could not claim;
But, here the antiquarians trace
The lone, neglected burial-place
Of Eneas' nurse—so long rank grown
With thorn and weed—almost unknown.

VI.

The pavement ways, where victors led
The vanquished, feel no more the tread
Of valor ; and, where chariots sped,
The pleading beggar kneels in dread,
Whose courage and whose hope are fled.
Grand, templed roads through groves of shade,
The debt of cold neglect have paid;
Where now a ride through dust awaits
Him who would gain Capua's gates;[4]

VII.

Near by, is pointed out, to-day,
The spot where dark assassins lay,
When jealous malice rashly made
To swiftly fall the flashing blade,—
O Rivalry! thy angry glow
So caused the burning stream to flow
Bright, from the heart of Cicero;
Than his, no truer lips were dumb,
When carried pale, to dreadful Rome,—
Antony's mandate was fulfilled;[5]
And sweetest silver tones were stilled.

VIII.

Proud cities are not nature's choice:
Her lavish hand, and stirring voice
Are seen and heard, beyond control
Of man, who fearless gains the goal
Of power—to lose his life—his soul.

IX.

If thou, Campagna, drear and lone ![6]
Shouldst lend this theme a saddened tone,
Whose wooden crosses, record keep,
Where all of life, and love, long sleep;
Thy darkened spirit's legendry.
In ruins of antiquity,
Majestic desert by the sea!
Is all, now left to time of thee.

X.

If, from the Aventine's crushed dome,[7]
Some civic leaves of laurel come,
Herein, they're newly wreathed. and sweet,

And laid along the pathless way,
By such child hands as dropped the wheat,
To mark where they were carried far;
Nor distant road, nor sun, nor star,
 Had any signal whence they'd come;
Of little woodland babes, one day,
Such tender story we are told,
Long after their own lips are dumb;
And never, meanings sweet, grow old.
The red feet of the Sylvan doves
That lit, and flew, and lit again;
That lit, and flew, and picked the grain,
And left no speck where it was cast;
Came out from shadows of the groves—
Came near where they were lying dead;
And seeing them locked cold and fast,
With russet leaves, light overspread
The plaintive sorrow of their fate,
So still, and pale, and desolate.

XI.

So thou, fair Cumaen Sibyl![8]
Lain dead for ages, may not will,
From soft shut eyelids and still breath,
To wake what fancy cherisheth.
The crisping flames that arches shook,
Consumed thy bright Sibylline Book;
And fleets may sail to Egypt's shore
For relics of the proud Cleo;[9]
But who shall find, for evermore,
That light, bright ashes, slumb'ring low?
O'er it the camel's feet may haste,

When going out towards Syria's waste;
And Arab idlers may sit down
On perished fragments of thy crown:
But Alexandrian fires have not
Burned the strange mystery of thy lot;
There lives some flower's perennial bloom,
To ever grow upon thy secret tomb.

XII.

Where Cypress groves, low murmur infinite
Sad requiems by fountains long left drear,
No more beside them may the Goddess sit
Nor sunlight, mid the marbles, shadows rear:
Rank, o'er their ruins, crowns of nettles grow,
Since Bayard's cruelties encompassed woe,
And left the lamentations of his crime.
Though cold the sterile majesty of time
Whose pale form moves with ceaseless, noise-
        less tread,
Where now no captive, stealthy foe beguiles;
Though springing mines are still; and lone
        defiles
Of dense Abruzzi, hide their lines of dead,
And bear soft echoes of the Alpine chime,
A dirge for desp'rate hopes so vainly led,
Through Parian caves, whose fine veins reveal
What flashed with luster of Canova's steel:—
O land of Prowess! there is still in thee,
The unsubdued, strong wrath of agony!
The oaks of Virgil, and Nisida's Isle;
The sunsets, from Miseno's hills, that smile

O'er burnished Jasper where the headlands
    lean,
Still, the traveler thrill.

XIII.

                  Where thou art seen,
Deserted Pisa! long each towering dome[10]
Has been, for butterflies and birds, a home;
And doomed consumptives seek thy balmy air,
To linger out sweet life, as fleet as fair.
The chiseled buttress of thy lone, vast walls,
To glory and its splendor, ne'er recalls;
And to thy litanies' austere restraint,
The seabreeze murmurs back responsive plaint.
Thy great Cathedral's jewels lie in gloom;
And all thy record is a costly tomb.
Fortress, and Pyramid, that Satraps raised,
May not with thee be classed, with thee be praised:
Grand Campo Santo's sculptured arches claim[11]
The birthplace of Historic art's pure fame:
Solid with stone, and solemn unto death—
Hope's immortality expressed to faith,—
The light of an existence beaming new,
In hollows of the deep grave brightness threw,
Symbol and sanctity in awe combine
The mystic halos of each pillared shrine;
And precious woods whose broad walls, varied
    gleam
With many brilliant shades whose colors seem
Iridescent with heaven's ambient beam,
Arched with the glory of its promise bow,
Where lit, a hundred lamps of worship glow;

Though in recumbent grace, or though they
    stand—
Brutus and Bachus in the silence grand,
Beside the holiness of truest Saint—
The moveless satire of time's secret plaint;
Effaced, or half effaced, the stones of script—
The cup long empty by the lamp of Crypt,
Long cooled upon its stand. O'er nameless dust,
The corselet of the warrior left to rust;—
As of Camillus, it is said, the wing
Of some light flutterer o'er meads, may fling
Renownless atoms on the summer air,
Borne by the winglet from such place of prayer;
The gorgeous festivals of Lupercal, [12]
With consecrated lights, no longer shall
Glow in the Pantheon; for, Candlemas—
The same—yet not the same, as that which was,
From myriad pagan gods, withdrawn to shine
O loved Madonna ! on that face of thine !
No motto graved on arch or cenotaph,
Portrays thy mystic, signal glory—half;
It is for trembling thoughts that dare aspire;
Though dedicated thou, the temple's fire
Blazed in the pathway of thy naked feet
Whose steps upon the ashes are complete—
Minerva and Sibyl have quenched tripods—
Thou, still the altar of the ancient gods.

CANTO SECOND.

The Carbonari.

I.

Out on the midnight tolled the bell—
Alerta sta—that all was well !
And, still was the air, and dim the sky
With the thick, dark mist that hung on high:
Nothing was heard but the tramping sound
Of slow steps timing the patrol's round:
The people's thoughts were as quiet wings
In careless trust of unconscious things;
Save only a dreamless, tested few
That in trembling dared—if false—if true;
To a large old building these had come,
Except for a password, seeming dumb.
The room was only a little square,
That well was seated when all were there;
And a strangely fashioned lamp burned bright,
Which brought this out by its ruddy light.

II.

They were a class from the best of men;
When gathered and reckoned, numbered ten;
And counted in age from twenty four

To forty, it might be, less or more;
With faces all that were strongly set,
Where purpose and will together met;
With glossy dark hair and foreheads large,
Where thought was held as a holy charge;
Whose unshaken faith imperiled fear,
Had heeded not when in meeting here:
To Titian these were a worthy band
For the pencil's toil of his gifted hand.

III.

All silent—not a sound of breath—
The room was still, as still as death:
At last, one slowly raised his head,
From leaning on his hand, and said
In solemn tone that trembled low,—
"Let us adjourn it, Brothers, so;
Because a revolution, dared
To failure, meets no hope's reward;
For only then inhuman shown
Were that which none would dare to own."
Then with a stern, face rose there one
Who said: "Nay, now too much is done!
This, the land of Sicily's sons,
Of mountain caves, and burried guns;
The stealthy Sbirro found them not
Where long since they were left to rot:
Deep from their rust they're taken up
To fill with blood the Bourbon cup;
I know you'll answer best in deed
What thus you would who hear and heed."

IV.

They rose at his inspiring word,
As though a wind a forest stirred:
Suppressed and slow, one spoke for all—
"This purpose we shall not recall.
If still, imperious repose
Abjures the will, let it disclose
The fainting doubt that strives, and guess
The furtive No or faithful yes"!
And "Yes" repeated ev'ry one—
That night's most secret pledge was done.

V.

Out paled the stars, stillness, and dews,
Dawn's manifest sweet interfuse;
And there Cozenza stood alone,
For each had passed, and all had gone.
He bared a white brow to the night, which shone
Like a drooped wing whose dove plumed peace had
    flown,
Or, the soft crest that at the sunrise lines
The morning sky of his own Apennines.
Is there some harmony of deepest close?
Or fine laid color of the sweet bloom rose?
A conscript sleeping ere the day he goes,
The void of outward things; the transient breath
Of kindling heaven; and the secret wrath
Of a wild river that breaks out from snows:
Yet, with that patience in his dark eyes deep,
As of some pain long borne, and laid to sleep.
Such was Cozenza; and a vigil's flame

Burned in the very signal of his name—
A fettered triumph, and a scepter's claim.

VI.

Half rounded was the wall, and ten feet high,
Where nine devoted men were led to die;
At base of Pellegrino—Ciardone—
A plain beyond the city, vast, and lone,
Excepting a stone bench, altar, and seat—
Where last prayers were said, fearless, and fleet.
'Twas there Cozenza's father, shot to death,
With fortitude's last hour and love's last breath,
Adjured the son beloved, with heritage
Whose light illumined all life's after page
With high intent, and firmest rectitude;
The efforts of high aims, not understood
As yet, by that fair boy, who wept and heard
As one who stood in caves where thunder stirred.
Half conscious of his sad impending loss,
Through corridors so sloping, tortuous,
Far down before a key had turned the door,
Whose gloomy entrance was a prison cell;
Where dawn scarce lightened night one little hour:
Stricken and drooping, like a storm drenched flower,
The child was gently led to this farewell.

VII.

And soon, the dear embrace that held him close,
Had calmed his young heart's anguish to repose:
The grief of love's despair, first, last, once more,
Had stamped that tender heart indellible—
There, within clammy walls whose dungeon light

Was toned to quail a malefactor's blight.
The low vault roof, the straw strewn floor, and
   stool,
The only furniture allowed by rule,
Except a lantern that unsteady swung,
And wavered when, with clang, the door was flung:
Here, mournful and intent, the dying sire
A martyr's holy faith, would still inspire:
Soulfelt and whispering the while with joy,
"Be as a father, to thy brothers, boy,
And, to thy stricken mother, gentle e'er,
Bereaved so bitterly, sustained by pray'r;
Unsullied be the name I leave to thee;
Keep it, rememb'ring efforts yet to be,
The watchword of a trial's darkest sea—
A standard for thy country's liberty."

VIII.

So died that hero; and two decades gone,
Cold grew the horror of the deed long done;
And colder, the sweet eyes that wept for him,
Some years since veiled with yew trees, and grown
   dim,
That widowed mother of majestic grief—
As for the rest, it is all less and brief;
The confiscating spoiler's claim was rife,
And left Cozenza but a restless life.
At times, he visited the stony shrine,
To keep hope definite, not to repine.
There still the bullet holes struck in the wall,
Or, there a mourning peasant to recall

The recollections long revered with dread,
And teach his son to name the honored dead,
While half unmindful of the stranger, near,
Who loved to hear him, whom he need not fear,
Though telling how, again the noble land
Felt all the hated craft of Ferdinand.
And thus, Cozenza's manhood, sadly came
Through direst vengeance and ambitious flame:
Grand in his sorrow, in his purpose strong,
Bound as to Sethon, to his life that wrong.[13]
With anger ninefold, and a father lost—
His young reflections on mad billows tost—
An orphan boy forgotten, until when,
One more than *nine*, he made the secret ten,—
The faithful, trusted ten who understood,
And pledged their service in Abruzzi's wood.

CANTO THIRD.

The Sylva of the Dead.

I.

There was no rest: the awful night,
Was full of death's wan, stricken blight:—
The dreadful Plague held carnival;
Not heeding couch, nor cup, nor pall,
Nor rank, nor age, nor station—all
Afflicted, fair Palermo wept
In sadness, and death vigils kept.
The dead-cart rolled—the ready grave
Was all a victim hoped to have.
"Bring out your dead," the ghoulish cry;
Or "haste! come on! don't wait to die"!
The fiendish glance—the curse—the laugh—
Told not the horror all—nor half;
Else, strict, wide, silence, just not dumb,
But wakeful faintly with the hum
Of moans, that followed still a moan—
From distance come, to distance gone:—
The closing bang of rough box lids—
The cry,—the stillness that forbids

To question what was shut in there;—
The driver's oath—the mourner's pray'r—
Mingled upon the midnight air,—
One scarce the city, now could know,
So changed by one short month of woe.
Bright little shops, and houses closed;—
Death's squalor there alone reposed;
And, that the dead might burried be,
Were hated criminals set free.

II

Holding a phial's strong perfume,
The priest and doctor strode through gloom,
Conferring formal rites to die,
Reserved to special ministry;
And other adjutants were there,
Besmeared with dirt—with matted hair;
And arms, and legs, and feet, left bare;
These carriers of the dead, bestowed
In careless haste, each added load;
And with some gaudy finery laid,
A hideous derision made:
Each dirty rag, or falling shred,
Was mixed with plunder from the dead;—
Fine silks, embroidered vests, and coats,
Deep satin ties round grimy throats,
And fingers sparkling full of rings—
O'er all a frightful aspect throw,
Wierd contrast with life's flitting show:—
The crowded cart of senseless woes,
One more or less thrown in, ne'er knows;

Then Charon in another flings—
All ready, mounts his seat, and sings.
Grieving, a voice was heard to say,—
"Here is one dead! stop, come this way"!
And, at a window opened, shown
A maiden's face fair, and alone.

III.

Her mournful eyes now tear-stained, late were
    bright
With earnest smiles that beamed like rays of light;
Of the fairest race, she was beauty's own,
Her brow like a lily that night is on,
Her delicate lips of Raphael curve.
Had the lucid vein and tremulous nerve,
Pliant with power's mysterious being—
It is not described, you know it when seeing.
In play of the wind, moved her soft, dark curls;
Her hand was the sign of a thousand Earls—
Though I write this in a Republic land,
There are many here who will understand,—
We are still like those who have gone before us,
This rule holds good since old Heliodorus:
And no matter what transmigrated shore is,
The destiny of a wandering race,
It is still the same, through all time or place;—
And when I have mentioned her teeth of pearls,
I've told of one of the prettiest girls,
And a Neapolitan home and name
Of the proudest and noblest, she might claim.

IV.

What did she there alone ? what did she there ?
This being, like a flower, strange and fair;
Escaping, while she dared the pestilence—
Her low voice on the night—the darkness dense,
Except the fitful torches here and there,
That paled in vapors of the midnight air ?
Oh ! she was not alone:—in anguished pray'r
Her mother sobbing, knelt upon the floor,
With bended head, too prostrate to adore;
And here, with dread abandon of great grief,
The father lay in death,—sad, cold relief!

V.

The mother trembled to a gentle touch,—
"O grieve not, mother; nay, why weep so much ?
If we should leave for Naples ere the sun,
Think where we are, and all that must be done :
An English brig will leave Messina—and—
You may, or will you write to Ferdinand ?"
She hesitated in emotion, as
Though she had thought of more, and let it pass.
" My child speak on, I know what you would say;
I do not care to haste, nor, make delay,
Indifferent, let fate bring what it may.
Ah ! yes; I know the rest; your anxious face—
This hour restraining love, hath still its grace;
For you, my dear, I scarce know what to do,—
We go to San Gregorio Armeno:
My cousin, the good Abbess, will to thee

Extend her cautious care, months two, or three:
There I will leave thee, till returned again—
Some pension from the king I must attain. "—
Downcast, Etolia listened; and silent, did remain.

VI.

Here three men entered, and the converse ceased:
One of them, seeming a St. Francis priest;
From all quarters in a ritual book,
The trusted monks, dread correspondence, took.
Father Caldara, being one of those—
A patriot too, despite the calm repose
Of pious law—a faithful priest withal,
Fervently ready unto duty's call,
He cared not.for the pestilential breath—
Despair had nought for him; and life, no death;
And passing, where the Plague flag's yellow furl
Waved o'er the mother and the watchful girl,
Had entered neath its death-like shadows low;
He had known Olevano long ago—
De Olevano, noblest Count that e'er
Sued to tyrant king, a patriot's prayer;
Suspected, to be disaffected, long,
Patient, he waited the redress of wrong,
Through dull, inactive years of want and pain.—
At length, to royal favor once again,
Too late restored, by effort that obtained
The service that his rank and worth, had claimed:
A far Calabrian Governor, the meed
Appointed by the king unto his need.
Now he lay dead; no voice to wake him more:

Daughter, and wife, alone the loss deplore—
For nurse, and servants all had died before.

VII.

In upper hills of Naples, gorge and dell,—
With cloud-lit splendors that above them swell;
Close to sweet, small Lesila's olive groves—
Were Olevano's towers, filled with doves;
And silent halls, and splendid spacious rooms,
And remnants of the past, and lonely tombs
Of ancestry.

VIII.

But now they could not place
Him placidly to rest—could not retrace
Their journey there. Alas, so far away
From their unrested hope that stricken day,
The proud, old Castle Olevano lay ;
Quiet and grand, the sleeping hills among;
While o'er its lord, the pall of death was flung—
Not now at least; but with the Sylva's dead,
Strangers—and many—there, he must be laid:
Delays, and journeys, and the quarantine—
So far, his distant home—these were between.

IX.

Unto the Sylva, then they took him:—Fate[14]
Had no alternative; and desolate
Was night, a night of sorrow—the hour late—
They took him, mourning, without pomp or state;
Alike, that dreadful time, to poor and great,
Was the remorseless Plague's insatiate frown.

"In upper hills of Naples, gorge and dell,—
With cloud-lit splendors that above them swell;
Close to sweet, small Lesila's olive groves—
Were Olevano's towers, filled with doves;
And silent halls, and splendid, spacious roooms,
And remnants of the past, and lonely tombs
Of ancestry."

Page 38.—Stanza VII.

The glorious moon in splendor streaming down
On gardens long, and by-paths in the trail
Along which moved the cortege; and the pale,
Bright stars came out to gem the concave vale:—
The wind's wild wail, through bending boughs
    made sound
Of music, to the shadows on the ground:—
Except a woman's grieving widowhood,—
All listless, the centurial Cypress wood
Far out against the sky like watchers stood;
And the lone patrol, on his nightly round,
Whose footsteps moved the silence—else profound.

X.

Close to the iron gate, they entered by,
Was a small pillar, pointing to the sky,
Which, frescoed paintings of the Passion, showed,
Or, how the burning fires of Hades glowed:—
Then a square grating to an under vault,
At turning of some Avenue, was caught:—
Sad glimpses all, though beautiful the scroll
Which in the silv'ry moonlight o'er them stole;
And there, through vacant spaces of the trees,
A Gothic Chapel's soft, illumined peace :—
Here to the Sylva, when the dews were deep,
The few had come to bury him, and weep.

XI.

Another there had come: what was his quest?
Was he a watcher in that place of rest?
Why started he, when drew the cortege near ?
Was he a waiting mourner of the bier ?

Or had the anxious thought, that often glooms
The soul, enticed him forth among the tombs?
The wheeling bat flew by him, and away;
Restless, he moved where darker shadows lay,
And sadly mused:—

        "O life, thou art a day!
Behold, how many great and noble sleep,
Within these spacious vaults, that silence keep!
Hark! the cemetery bell—the lone hour
Of midnight in the mountains! dismal power!
Rebounding, echoes from each distant place!
O man! one hour is past—one more to trace!
Happy is he who has no cause to fear
The hour of destiny approaching near.
Yea, mourning women! whom I watch, unseen,
Sad emblems of my country! do you lean
Your broken hearts upon a broken reed?
Let Faith and Hope inspire despair's great need!"

XII.

Thus mused Cozenza; until thought was staid
By a light hand upon his shoulder laid.
"Delay not" said the low voice—he obeyed.
"Caldara! Friend and Father! is it you?
I have waited here some hours in the dew.
Are they all down there now?" he sudden grew
More cautious still with this inquiring tone,
And glanced to see were yet the mourners gone.
"Who are *they*?—Are they strangers? Do you
   know?
What news? and tell me quickly, speaking low."

XIII.

"What news, and who are *they?* sad news at best:
There lies Count Olevano at his rest;
And *there*, his wife and daughter desolate;
And, since a few days, hapless is the strait
Of fair Messina, filled with ships of fate—
The devastating troops are landing in
Carnage most terrible, and ruin's din—
The people of Messina fly to us—[15]
Our two battalions are a total loss !—
Boys, twenty, and sixteen, how well sustained,
Unflinchingly, and long—the heart is pained;—
Out of two thousand, there returned, but eight;
Presenting to the Ministry, they said:
'Behold, and count us ! all the rest are dead!
Here is our Banner, and heed not our fate !—
Though red the waters of Messina run,
And we were slaughtered,—is its honor won.' "

XIV.

"Does Countess Olevano know I'm here ?
To fair Etolia speak before you go;
And, if she know not, you may let her know,
And tell our friends below, that I am near !
I knew all that you told me of the fleet,
And fighting at Messina.   It is meet,
Some care be taken of those ladies—chance
Alone must grant them safe deliverance;—
Because the English Brig, no refugees
Will take on board, until a day of peace."

XV.

The grieving Countess had to pray'r withdrawn,
To wait within the little church, till dawn;
Her child's low converse with the friendly priest—
Anxiety or thought, cost not the least:
It was, no doubt, some gentle care they planned
Of morning journey, and to understand
Who should companions be.

XVI.

　　　　There was no lamp;
The moon, alone, lit all the heavenly camp.
Etolia listened! Ah what soft, light step?—
Her lips were parted; and her breath was deep—
There in half shadow, there, before her stood—
Yea, he had come! and dark the Cypress wood;
And white the low Verbenas on the ground
Beside his pathway, silent, most profound.
He was her own : the aerial glow
And her own frightened heart, his name might know.
She did not greet him with her joy or woe;
But took his hand, saying or sighing, oh!
What things he said—his sweet and fond embrace—
Would here in passive words find little trace.
What efforts then she made with tremors cold,
That swift her startled thoughts to him be told—
His kisses oft—Ah me! the story old—
And yet, forever good, like perfect gold.

XVII.

Would she go to Carmine? there he held
Apostolato sittings.　Numbers swelled

Daily, the ranks of the devoted few,
Whose fervent destiny more brightly grew ;
And her own happiness more sweetly true.
Nay, it were vain to ask king Ferdinand,
Consent to e'er bestow on him her hand;
Too deep endorsement of suspected taint
Would seal her father's mem'ry with complaint :
Her loving mother's need—the kingly ire,
Were she to wed a Lib'ral, adding fire
To what had been alleged against her sire.

XVIII.

While ling'ring, loving, grieving, waited they,
The hours delayed not the approaching day.
Passive and mute, with resignation won,
She had with effort felt that all was done—
He had departed with the waning moon.—
Pale, as the Ivory statue of Alea,
She stood, forgetful he was not still near.—
The night wind blew ; but not the Sylva's dead
Heard the sweet words that he had fondly said :—
She murmured ;

XIX.

   "O my God ! thy will be done ;
As a wrecked swimmer on the waters thrown,
My hope is at thy mercy—thine alone !
Ah ! now to me, it has been well revealed,
That thy dear presence inaccessible,
Hid in the tempest, like a cloud-wrapt sun,
Is that to which my soul should have appealed,
Changeless forever, without human spell—

Of eyes whose look is a vain agony,—
Of lips whose beauty is a silent wail;
These have no story e'er to tell to me—
Those shade their splendor in thy Temple's vail!"

XX.

On her foot, was placed the slipper of glass;
She could not stand up when her Prince did pass;
The spindle was touched; and the Princess slept—
And lowly, Etolia knelt down, and wept.

XXI.

O mystic Love! Why, in thy sense of soul,
Is some pain perfect to usurp control?
A gentle Wolf that walks within the wood;
A little one who knows not ill from good,
Whom we remember by her crimson hood—
Her hapless Grandma not more wise than she,
Ages on ages keep their legendry:
Forever, is the latch unlifted—yet,—
We see, with consternation and regret,
Outside, the Wolf and Riding Hood still wait:
Inside, the Grandmother bewails her fate—
All this—for sake of Love we would forget.
Still, Mustapha's son the mystery tries:
The Lamp is touched to luster with surprise,
While countless gems flash out before his eyes:
Elate with pride and hope, ambitions blend;
And a black mountain, and its caverns end
The journey where the Genii descend.

CANTO FOURTH.

The Catacombs.

I.

Follow Cozenza, where the colored panes
Chequered the somber light with many stains,
Around the Chapel, to another door;
Entering, unobserved as all before,
He looked around, and saw he was alone.
At one end, was an altar of gray stone,
Surmounted by a heavy cross of wood
That for a century upon it stood:
Short rows of benches leaned against the walls,
Unpainted; and quaint biers with faded palls
That once were damask—even signal death,
Faded or graded, a tokened splendor hath.
Several pick-axes, and bars, and spades,
Lay in another corner—fun'ral aids.

II.

An oaken door led from the altar's left —
Downward a solid stairs that had been cleft
From rock.   Here faintest gleam of light had fled,
And made more cautious each descending tread.

Thus downward, making steps and pathway sure,
He reached the second narrow sepulture,
Which being dark, he stumbled o'er a skull,
Or ran against the niches that were full
Of ghastly inmates, till he turned a third
Long gall'ry—saw a light, and voices heard.
Here, too, an altar, and some seats of stone,
Used by the Monks at pray'r in days long gone;
Once more the Comitato's tested few,
Welcomed their daring leader, tried and true.

III.

Father Caldara, and some twenty more,—
One of them went to guard the staircase door,
The others seated on the benches, round,
Attentive silence, pending and profound,
Secret and pledged, an anxious, waiting Band—
All sworn enemies to Ferdinand.
Those men of Fate! O Palmerston! what use[16]
Your crafty policy and futile snares?
They dared and suffered, though you did refuse
The promised aid to their relying prayers.

IV.

Caldara stood with foot upon the stair
Of the lone, long forgotten altar, where,
Within a little nook, a lantern's gleam
Made all the gloomy shadows denser seem,
But lighting earnest thought in ev'ry beam
Of soulful eyes there gathered, though but few,
Brave leaders all, of mountain peasants who,

Would die with them, when they their lances drew.
Sworn on the skull and crossbones lying there,
Cozenza's left hand resting on them—bare;
Emblems of Death most awful, just, severe,
Not signs of failure, slavery, nor fear.
" Son of the martyred dead! Hath the hour come?
Fulfill thy chosen vow, accept thy doom!
Here we have gathered from the cities far,
To guide our liberties beneath thy star:
Marked is the glass; and falling grain by grain,
Our citizens; our hopes, our efforts, vain !
Here to concert—then, let the trial be;
ITALIA UNA, AND OUR LIBERTY!"

V.

"Brothers! invested with your sternest trust,
E'en as a breastplate in the bloody dust,
With hope's collectedness I take the task;
And with what dangers fraught, I do not ask.
Of old, the dusty banner in this vault,
The breeze of Freedom on the sunshine caught;
And well you know that ev'ry shining blade
Must be a victor's or a martyr's, laid
Upon its crumbling fold,"—this, all he said.
" We do, we swear it," and they all arose;
As a storm lightens when a rainbow glows,—
So flashed their eyes, and clashed their saber blows.
But lo! that moment from the gallery's end,
What instant terror does that voice portend ?
" O fated men ! low hangs the tyrant's sword:
Light be your footsteps—silent ev'ry word:

Sbirri are knocking at the Sylva's gate:[17]
We must not fall alive—defend your fate!
Fierce Maniscalco's minions trapped you here—
If we *must* fall, our blood shall cost them dear."

VI.

" Be calm," Caldara said; "this shock to meet;
Stir not, though time is precious, minutes fleet."
Approaching a side niche, he touched a spring,—
Though not performing in the highland fling—
The standing occupant around did swing,
Disclosing an apperture into which
They scarce could pass, man after man. The niche
Revolved back to its place with ringing sound;
And in a grotto, then, themselves they found,—,
Not more than eight by ten, in height or size;
Of unaccustomed darkness to their eyes;
So damp and chill the air, their blood would freeze;
But stirred by dire alarm, and ill at ease
With great excitement—there was little thought
Of cold or damp—such things were held as nought.

VII.

"Hasten!" said Caldara; " because, if they
Perceive with certainty we gathered here;
And that there is not an apparent way
For our escape,—I doubt not; and I fear,
They'll knock down all the dead, until they meet [18]
The secret spring discov'ring our retreat."
Dismal the grotto, though the lantern's light
They still had with them, taken in their flight.

Speechless they hurried; winding farther in
To where the deeper depths of Earth begin;
With many turnings, and at times ascending,
Contracting, narrowing, then downward tending
Where chisel marks were seen, and showed that man
Had made it wider, where it was a span.
Some spacious caverns were adorned with bright,
Fantastic, basalt rocks, and chrysolite,
And hanging stalactites that sparkled high,
Like emeralds, or diamonds, or the sky
When from the milky-way, star-studded light
Beams down resplendent on a summernight.
In other places they were stifled, by
A lack of air, and felt about to die,—
When from the creviced mountain, just above,
A breeze came wafted like a message dove,
Restoring them to vigor once again.
Two miles of weary way were traversed, when,
Like hunted harts, each tired, listening ear
Heard sound, of falling water somewhere near—
A subterraneous cataract, pent
Within the strata, until finding vent,
Where throes of Earth, the shaken rocks, had rent,
It foamed the cavern in its mad descent.

VIII.

The sounds increased, as on they nearer drew;
Smoother the path—; the cavern larger grew:—
More damp, and cool, and fresh, the air that blew.
Concealed by mist and foam, a passage lay,
Which should be crossed before the break of day:

A sheet of water, falling from a hight
Some fifteen feet, was dashing, foamy, bright,
Over a second fall, or precipice,
With noise tremendous into an abyss:—
They stopped in blank amaze when nearing this.
Irresolute, a moment there they stood;—
The path so sloping neath the frenzied flood,
Of swift descending water, now they viewed:—
One step, made false—were sure vicissitude.

IX.

Caldara first, with staff, went carefully;
Cozenza held his belt, and turning, he
Admonished order and attention—last,
Each clasped the other's hand, and safely passed.
" Here, now for needful rest,—you may abide;
I'll watch, the while you sleep," the faithful guide
Said thoughtfully, of their so late fatigue.
They rested; and, when silence on them came,
Cozenza's restless thoughts were on the League;
And, seeing that they slept not, he might claim
Their aid discussing the new action's plan.
It was so then devised, that ev'ry man
Should form a Cormitato's separate ten,
Each one of whom in turn to other men [19]
Should bond and secret of the League impart,
But not the intimation of its start;
Thus strictest secrecy's profound regard,
Compelled as safety's watch, and faithful ward—
Even inflicted torture could not claim
Knowledge of more than one, such leader's name.

And, being in this way, confined to few,
Betrayal could not harm the whole League through.
Caldara's monks might traverse all the towns—
Free of suspicion were their holy gowns;
What subtile strength ulterior motive tries;
Thus Freedom's strongest allies in disguise,
With ardent zeal, would aid the enterprise.

X.

The sun had now illumed the morning skies;
And softly splendid were his gorgeous dyes,
Astream the vale, where sweet Palermo lies;
Halting, they found themselves upon a mount—[20]
Four miles of weary distance they might count
Outside Palermo, since the painful night
Of danger's chance and terror's secret flight.
Close by, a splendid frescoed, ruined wall
Stood in sublime decay.   Here parting all—
Cozenza counselling, their parting led,
And with impressive words in fervor said;
" Here part we in the name of God;
The peasants soon will be abroad,
And take strange note of what we do—
This lonely place is full in view—
The town of Morreale, each
Alone, an hour hence, may reach:
The patrols then will have retired—
Keep bright the hope, so late inspired—
Farewell ! Farewell! our oaths retain."
Some of them never met again.

XI.

Return we to Etolia, where she wept,
And all the long, long night its vigil kept;
And vainly did her thoughts like billows toss,
Lamenting, more than ever, true love's loss.
She dared not ask a mother's grief to share
The woe that burdened her with keen despair;
But strong relief in pray'rful words she sought;
And thus alone poured out each anguished thought.
"Thou wilt forget me in my cheerless lot, .
Cozenza, my beloved!—wilt thou not?
O God! he will forget in hope's decay,
Though I may love, and watch, and weep, and pray;
Oh I must love thee, through all ill and blame,
Though bitter fountains of mine anguish threw
Some drops upon the bright fire of thy name,
Still wert thou tender unto me, and true;—
Beloved! forever let it be the same.
A fate is on me, friend—thy tribute sent—
And from my grief insep'rate—thy intent!
Have I not won of thee some pow'r to bless
My longing heart? to triumph o'er distress?
Father in Heaven! only thou canst send
The light upon the darkness. till the end!
My youth glides from me like a forest stream,
Darkly, and far, without the sunlight's gleam;
But once, through kindling boughs, thy love shone
    down,
And lightened my lone soul with rapture's crown:
What dews of other paths, my life may keep,
Thy one, blent, burning stream flows to its deep.

As grieved Properzia Rossi cut the veins
Of marble, to a lovely image wrought,
So would I, in the future's sweet refrains,
Leave closes of the strain thy love hath taught;
Something of me to live, for that bright sake,
Where other hearts may learn to live and break;
For this my heart shall know sublimities,
Under the fiery struggle overcome,
Loving in patience till I find its peace,
Like some deep, placid stream far from its source
Of broken spray, dashed rocks, and rushing foam,
Grown into calm, bright beauty on its course."

XII.

"My child, why linger long, and sadly here;
Last eve you were the comforter, thy clear
And patient eyes, defying sleep and woe!
Come with me! Leave this place of death!" and low
The gentle mother drew upon her breast,
The drooping head she tenderly caressed.
"Tell me what painful thoughts have so distressed
Of late thy chastened spirit? child so dear;
Confide them to thy mother without fear!
Thy father's death? 'tis more! I see it swell
Thy troubled bosom, like a restless spell.
When home at Olevano wilt thou tell
The secret sorrow to my heart, so well
Thy place of fond repose, thy refuge e'er,
Dove of my lonely life?—and now prepare!
The Cardinal Capano will return
With us to Naples." Ere the sun did burn
The sky at noon-day, they were on their way—
Haste and discomfort, not more than delay.

CANTO FIFTH.

The Banditti.

I.

Those classic roads of *"Auld lang Syne,"*
Well known beyond all pen of mine,
Where poor Lipari saltworkers
Came out, and did a few things worse
Than gath'ring salt, (I mean of course)—
They e'en ignored a Cardinal's curse,
While going for his watch and purse ;
Or held him till a ransom came,
As eminent, as his Eminence' name.
Although this way they often risked disasters,
The pay was much more than a few piasters,—
The scanty earnings of a toilsome day,
On which they scarce could live.

II

      The sunlight's ray
Is needed that a flow'r may bloom in play
Of golden winds.   The fervor of man's heart
Is governed by condition—to depart

From brilliancy of purpose—high intent;—
And, wilted, faded, bloomless, oft is bent
To blight's ignominy.   A human life
Is but a gladiator in the strife
Of toil's arena.   But where softly blows
The garden full of perfumes, round the rose,
Perceptible the influence ; and soon,
It lifts its balmy sweetness to the glows
Of morning, and of evening, and of noon.
The one, with effort, may still find defeat :
The other, cannot help but to be sweet,—
If this be palliation, let it be
Atonement for the men of Lipari ;
And cite the judgments of defying caste—
There still, must be a first, and still, a last.
This is as it should be: but the extremes,
Like torrents confluent, from rippling streams,
That in their separate beauty might be fair,   ·
Submerge and overwhelm all, with despair

III.

So; Capano being a Cardinal,
With carriages, outriders, in fact, all
Appurtenances of religious rank;—
The other fellows hid behind a bank,
Desp'rate with poverty's oppression,—lank
And lean with woful want,—inheriting the land
Of famed Tiberius—infamous Ferdinand:
We cannot pardon—but we understand
Why ev'ry second man is a Brigand:
Rough fragments of the bright Brait's edges they—

Still gems, though cut from the great gem away.
Capano heard the Countess' tale of woe,—
Having arrived that morn from Reggio,
And passing onward to a distant port;—
He thus could give the ladies his escort.
Small boats were anchored where the Islands lay ;
To these, their journey easy, day by day,
Just taking needful rest along the way ;
Avoiding all the ills of civil strife
That darkened Naples, and Palermo life.

IV.

Capano was Caldara's uncle; that,
Accounts for things not mentioned--—but apparent ;
He had received the news from this knight-errant: '
As for the rest—he was good natured,—fat,
A loyal, pious, old aristocrat,
Unconscious of his nephew's lib'ral views—
An old friend of the Count de Olevano,
Of whom, the late demise was startling news,
And much deplored by Cardinal Capano.
But now his friendly aid—the journey taken
Had interruption rude, and cause to waken
Their thoughts from the late grief, and future plans,
When captured, as they were, by the Brigands.

V.

They had gone onward to the mountains, east,
That circle half the city from the north—
But now no hope of being soon released.
A special ransom, was Capano worth ;

And prudently, that morning he had come—
His journey needed but a trifling sum—
He could not, therefore, pay it then, but waited;
And loudly, the bandits, meanwhile berated.
We dwell not in Etolia's deep distress;
And for her sake, her mother's not the less;—
Soon they were hurried to a mountain cave,
With such respect and gallantry as have
A blended heritage in man's strong heart,
Even when chance and time have driven apart
The agitated links of tender thought,—
Which love maternal, earlier had taught,—
Into distorted things all fiery wrought;
And melted idealities of youth,
Have paled to coldest iron bands of truth.

VI.

Salvator Rosa!. genius, who portrayed
The storm in the thick forest, that dismayed
Its utter silence; who, by stricken trees,
Waited to watch the lightning's mysteries
Transfix themselves in darkness, and the low
And thunder-trembled clouds blinding the glow;—
Serenity, not there; the sleep of gold
That heaves in the soft sunset—never told!
So had'st thou marked each darkly splendid face
Of desperate Salluzzi, and his band,
With painting's touch, some glory's mist to trace,
That lives in pathos, as another land.

VII.

Etolia trembling, softly walked beside
Her mother; closely veiled, as if to hide
Her grief renewed, and slightly fearful, as
A frightened child, who danger's paint must pass.
The Countess' passive pale hands sought her cross
And Rosary—"O child! had we not loss
And sorrow comfortless enough, that this
Deserveless fate of fortune we might miss?"
As the deep winds thrill over shattered chords,
The tremors of great grief disturbed her words ;
And on her wet, wan cheek of quivering pride,
The dignity and suffering vainly vied.
What said Etolia ?—little—she, too, wept,
Except some words ot hope, scarce firmly kept—
She clasped the cold and yielding hand, and led
Her mother slowly, with unlifted head.

VIII.

The home of the untoiling, free Brigand
Is, usually, the same in ev'ry land :—
From Meteora's grassy, hollow hills.
To where the shadow of Ciphissus thrills
The caves that Phidias cleft;—the tumbled stone
Of gloried, lonely, ancient Selinon;[21]
And near the tomb-built chamber of Theron:—
There the black steed is tied ; and there the base
Of some weed-covered column, serves as place
For the repast at noon,—the short light sleep
That, feared reprisal, keeps from falling deep.

IX.

Salluzzi Castrucci, was quiet, stern;
And seemed not what he was,—one scarce would
   turn
To note him twice: the short unrippling tress
Of glossy sable, touched his forehead less,
Than the great shadows of his painful heart,
That o'er its blue-veined light, at times did start.
His hands were beautiful and small; and fleet
Might be his indolent and easy feet:
And much of latent strength and manly grace,
Endowed the robust shoulders. His sad face,
Despite the weariness upon it set,
Had brows like crescent night: a coronet
Could not have veiled his blue eyes' secret gloom,
Nor made the pale rose on his cheek to bloom.
He seemed, with nonobservance of things fit,
To be a king,—though he was a Bandit.
He gave, with certain orders and detail,
Word to send onward to Mazara's vale—
And there confine within Segesta's grot—
The noble captives that were lately brought;
That, all supliance of release, be nought,
Until the ransom should be paid, he sought:
And that, with all respect, and gentle care,
The ladies be conducted, safely there.

X.

Swartly and fierce, were many of the men,
Standing around a fireplace in their den:
Numerous bottles, claret and champagne,

The long and highly polished Board did stain;
And some, with broken necks, were spurted at
The irate Cardinal who struggling, sat
In a large leathern chair, raised on a cask.
" Give us your benediction:" they would ask;
"You're the holiest target that we've had ;—
And, master of festivities, old lad!
Don't kick; and we'll untie you by and by"
And here, some random cork would hit his eye.
Thus did, their festal time, the hours prolong
With toast, and revel; careless wit, and song;
For not till midnight, would they journey take
To old Segesta, over dale and brake—
And this, was only one of eight or ten
Lone mountain caves, resorted by these men:
Across a winding passage, was another,
And smaller chamber, warmly tapestried:
The chiseled rock, by soft rich hangings hid.
This was assigned Etolia and her mother,

XI.

The loving daughter, here again essayed
The task of comforter; with art, portrayed
The rest and rescue, a few patient days
Would bring.   The moonlight's fall of silver rays
Fell on the divan where the Countess lay:
The daughter marked the hours ere coming day,
And then, the pillow, changed another way;
And, when with weariness the mother slept,
More easy grew the watch Etolia kept.
Near, was a window, or the rifted stone,

Through which the pale and purple starlight shone,
Need we to tell to loving hearts that muse,
What name, did then upon her thoughts infuse
Its deep, o'ermastering power? One more look,
To see if any wakeful tremor shook
The wearied mother lying now so still,
Resting, and sleeping fitfully. "She will
A moment miss me not ?"—self questioning;—
Just then, a nightingale let fall his wing,
And in the dusty thicket stayed to sing.
She longed to feel the outside perfumes fling
Their starlit ambience on her cheek's hot flush:
She rose; and, with examining light push,
Parted the folds of heavy tapestry,
Through which streamed down the brilliant,
    studded sky,
Disclosing interlacing shrubs and vines,
Around the rocks in delicate outlines;
And these dividing with her hands, she stood
One moment more in the deep underwood;
And faint, the mirthful din and robbers' shout,
Around the echo cave, came ringing out.
Standing in silence, ere she moved again,
Was that a woman's voice whose sweet refrain,
In that dread, lawless place, devotion sung,
With love's forgiving and impassioned tongue ?—
Amid the revel, strangely, sweetly clear
Its *awful sympathy fell* on her ear.

XII.

SONG OF THE BANDIT'S BRIDE.

" Oh at a leaflet's breath to start,
   And listen for thy step;
When from the mountain's rifted heart,
   The torrent floweth deep !

" Oft wild and weary coming back,
   Not bough, nor wave, nor air,
Breathes aught of crime, or danger's track,—
   Concealing danger's snare ?

"Upon the night, my soul would melt,
   Though dark seawinds have scorn ;
Thy scattered leaves of rose, I felt ;
   My heart kneels on its thorn.

" When in some mountain's hollow crest,
   No banner's noble fold
To wrap thy bleeding, dying breast,
   Thou'rt lying lone, and cold :

" Or when from danger's daring tryst,—
   My happy footsteps sped,
As oft to meet thee,—ah, when missed ;
   They carry thee in dead !

" O mountain rover ! this thy love
   That reaches unto grief !
Thou canst not fly ! O wounded dove !
   O starlight bright and brief !

"Thou art not sunlight, though on high
   Thou burnest pure and true ;
O wounded dove ! thou canst not fly
   From where the arrow flew !"

XIII.

The song was over , and she waited still,
To feel its after silence' tender thrill—
And half unconscious, till a quick faint wail
She heard, and hastened through the shrubbery's
   vail,
Into the rocky chamber. Oh what sight
Before her eyes ! or did she see aright ?
She did not know Salluzzi from the rest,
But by the star and dagger on his breast ;
And *Ave Maria* ! beside it pressed
Her lovely mother's white and stricken face
On which remained the cast of beauty's grace—
One startled moan ! she flew to her dear place :
With incoherent questions answered not,
Even, the intruder's presence, she forgot—
Chafing the languid hands, and kissing them,
With sobbing words of bitterest self-blame,
And calling often, on her mother's name.

XIV.

Salluzzi, who till now half leaned, half knelt,
Back on the pillow, gently laying down
The fair form from which life seemed to have flown,
Upon the forehead and the slight wrist, felt;
And knitting his dark brows, his glance grew stern

With pains appeal to that, not coming back—
The soul; decided, and resistless thing,
That, ere departing, lingered, fluttering—
The eyelids that would ne'er again upturn—
The pale small lips' strange speeches, murmurings—
Asking, where was she? on what unknown track?
Then once more folding, like two weary wings,
And falling into short and broken sleep:
And thus the slow, long night away did creep;
Salluzzi staid—seeing Etolia weep :—

XV.

"Maiden, thou dost not ask wherefore nor why
Thy gentle mother is about to die?
If I should let it happen, saying nought,
Thy misery would be more and overwrought.
She will recover, for a little while,
To reassure thee with her tender smile;
To do me justice, and to tell to thee
What e'er she wills of this night's mystery."
" Alas my mother! she can bear no more!
Though anger or surprise my heart o'er come,
My lips before thee, Chieftain, still are dumb.
If I withhold reproach I do implore
The cause of this: I own thy fearful power—
And yet, reliance place on thee, this hour."

XVI.

" Maiden, I knew thy mother ere thy birth;
She was the one I loved the best on Earth:
But, as I loved her, even so, thy sire

Made her the star of his one hope's desire—
He won her—for his name and rank were higher.
Her proud parents turned the wavering scale;
What was her yielding will—my woe's avail:
I wandered: and the sun and moon seemed fire:
And never, since that day, did hope aspire.
Behold she lived for him—O beauteous girl!
Fair was she, like thee—lip, and eye, and curl;
But now, there lying, like a faded pearl
Lost from its setting; after many years,
She gives to me her death, and memory's tears.
I knew her when your captors brought her here;
She saw not me; I did not then appear;
For what has happened, I had prescient fear:
And wouldst thou not that it should be alone
With none to witness it?—That trembling moan
Fortells that she revives—I will be gone."

XVII.

The Countess never lifted her closed eyes:
Her murmuring lips gave incomplete replies.
Until three days were past: then Death, more light
And merciful, than life's long weary blight,
Released the patient sufferer. She died
In the lone cavern by the mountain side.
Let us pass by the nearest days that came
To poor Etolia: they were as when flame
Is quenched by smoke; but ever hath relief
Come unto youth in time—what e'er the grief.

*5

CANTO SIXTH.

The Marriage in the Cavern.

I.

A horse of noble strength, and grace ;—
A rider on a high sloped place ;
Whose beaten track for way-farers—
Led on, to where sound rarely stirs ;
Far from the thicket's orange bush
Where night-birds thrill the evening's hush:
As nearer grew, the mountain range,—
Immersed, his thoughts, with event strange ;
Till on the summit, turned, to cast
A glance at the bright scene, he'd past.

II.

White Pyramids by Sulphur mines [22]
Made sunset break in silver lines;—
And golden gleams that shifting rose
And fell, like sudden firefly glows.
While thus absorbed, the awful sound,
"*Non Senti*," broke the stillness round !

If it was here, or there,—the shock,
He knew not: if behind the rock
A few feet distant—captors near,—
Then captive he, to bandits here.
He quick obeyed the dread command
To rein his horse, dismount, and stand!
In husky tones, each cruel word
And ruthless hand, he felt and heard.

III.

"*Ho*? *Ladro*! hand your money. here,
Or die! Wait not one moment's fear ;"
"Oh hang him now," one fellow said,
"Men tell no tales when they are dead!"
A dagger's point, his body felt ;
And, from its pressure, downward knelt:
He could not breathe, and lower lay
Where dust shut out the light of day.

IV.

Their careless hands his pockets tore,
Took watch and purse, and searched him o'er,
Until they thought he had no more.
The captive, struggling to regain
His strength and feet. did not complain;
But cried aloud with high disdain,
"What more you ask? What other call?
Release me now! you've taken all!
And, when to safety, I succeed,
I'll send you more—if more you need."
Then whispering some, they disagreed ;—

The scene another aspect wore:—
"I'll have it so!" the leader swore.
The captive trembling, heard; and then,
He found, his watch, put back again;
And, scarce believing, soon his purse
Replaced.   Again: the same voice terse,
As though from those lips, it were well
A cataract stay its thund'ring swell—
"A little while, move not: take heed!
Then mount your horse; and onward spee d:
Since now we leave you, look not back,
Till distant far, your traveled track:
A ball shall whistle through your brain,
If heedless, to my warning plain.
Now promise that you tell no tales."—
"I do," he answered, "What avails
To swear, because, I swear not ever?"
"Farewell!—I thank you—here we sever!"

v.

The bandit steps receded then—
The steps of more than twenty men;
And, when around the mountain side,
Their parting echoes faintly died:—
The captive rose from where he lay;
And mounted, rode he on his way.
His mind with trouble,—troubled yet—
But all things else—portmanteau set—
And strapped in faithful order, as
Before his venture in the pass:
Discordant, so the whole thing seemed—
His brain felt, as if he had dreamed.

VI.

Released, and once more on his way—
It now was near the close of day:
But, Hark! behind him hoofs astir!—
What sound upon the wind's swift whirr?—
A distant rider under spur—
Had he more venture to incur,
'Ere half a mile he scarce had gone?
Should he more swiftly hasten on?
The robbers had, on more debate,
Determined sure to end his fate?
With these foredoomed anxieties,
Instinctively, he onward flies;
And often strokes his startled horse,
And faster flies along his course:
To turn his head, he does not dare—
Remembering the warning fair—
He knew all that he had incurred,
And knew Banditti kept their word;
Not always, others—'tis averred,

VII.

In midst of his conflicting thought,
His path beside, a horseman sought:
"*Vive Maria!*"—soft salute,
"The night is beautiful and mute?"
"Yes; pleasant, very!" answered he;
"Is it less dangerous, if we
Ride on in friendly company?"
The dead leaf with the caverned wind;—
The sunset's glory, sealed and signed;

The roadway trouble, left behind;—
Now calmer, grew his startled mind:—
Not sullen watch, but guarded care
Imbued this cautious wayfarer.

VIII.

The stranger touched his falling plume,
In cautious speech, and did resume.—
"Have you seen any on this road?
And are you armed? if so:—'tis good?"
"What should one meet in this lone place,
But scenic beauty—nature's grace;
The solemn rock, the climbing goat,
The Cascade's falling sound, remote;
And as for arms,—why should I draw
Upon their strength? the firmest awe
That ever quickened fierce combat—
A conscience good—what more than that?
Menacing word,—foreboding sign,
Each terrible, majestic line,
Leads after this one line of law.
The beam which parts the dawning frown,
Will see me at the nearest town—
Know you? No! But, if right, I think,
As waters fall upon the brink
Of some familiar, fountain stone,
Beside which at some time I lay,
And watched the sky beyond its spray,
Your voice to me's a sound well known."

IX.

They now had reached a steeper hill
That rose upon their left.   The trill
Of some embosomed, woodland stream,
Fell softly on the ear;—a dream
Of peace, and moonlight, pure and calm,—
Transfixed, the cactus; drooped, the palm:
The loaded orange, golden pale;
The muleteers adown the vale ;
And old Segesta's Temples bare, [23]
Against the night, told where they were.
Here, the intruding stranger, showed
A path, which led from the main road,
Ascending, tortuous, and steep,
Where lay the rivulet asleep :
But in this fair Idalian grove,
Now sudden stopped the two, and strove.

X.

Quick as a flash,—as quickly flew
Our halted journeyer, and drew
A pistol from the saddle bow,
And fiercely eyed his unknown foe.
" Come now what will ! We're man to man !
This difference may change your plan ;
I do not mean to die, ere you
Find me avenged, and have your due !"
" Put by your weapon ! Had I thought
Of harm 'twere not your side I sought :
I am a friend, as you will see,
Ride close ! Ride on ; and follow me !"

XI.

Circuitous and narrow ways;
Ascending and descending maze,—
Where borders of a deep ravine
Above a shallow torrent lean :—
And here, the guide made him alight !
For now all things between them —right.
Who was he, for whom things amiss
Were thus made right, as seen in this?
I need not tell Cozenza's name,—
As he, to whom the stranger came;
I need not say the ambient cloud
Is gold, because the sun allowed;
Nor, that the trembling,.emerald sea
Is deep with troublous melody :
The stranger felt unworthily,
So great his own humility ;
But knew the leader of his land,
And scarce did dare to touch his hand—
While ready to go on, or stand,—
No true respect could greater be—
Such Brotherhood's Carbonari.
Thus he would live or die for him ,
And said, while tears his eyes did dim:—
" I know what you are ; and what I !—
You, live for right,—for wrong I die !"

XII.

His boots, hid in a thicket—lain
Concealed, he found a pair more plain :—
With pointed nails, the soles were set—

A man appeared, to whom, were let
The horses. Here the guide prepared
For perilous descent ; and shared
His steady foot-hold with his friend ;—
Down, slow, together, they did tend.

XIII.

Still on precipitous, and softly down ;—
At last, the torrent where a log was thrown,
Which made a passage to the other side—
Cozenza following his friendly guide.
Impenetrable rock, smooth, dark, and steep,
Where low shrubs, and the trees, deep vigils keep—
Once more, a rocky bank half way to climb,
And then Borghetto's tower tolled midnight chime.
At this lone spot, the guide with sure intent
Parted a heavy bush, that lowly bent,
Revealing entrance to a grotto.   Clear
He whistled; and a noise inside was heard
In answer; and an undistinguished word—
And drawing of a bolt by some one near.

XIV.

His shoulder then he placed against the rock,
And slowly turned it with a little shock.
On ent'ring, back the stone rolled into place,
And on the night outside left not a trace. ·
" Salluzzi is it you ?" a woman's voice
Said, half in fear, too anxious to rejoice.
" Yes, good Concetta! Did Lavagna come,
And bring his prisoner ? How have you cared

The lady sorrowing and orphaned late?
Here is a guest.   Give him the silken room ;
And let a costly supper be prepared."—
At all of this, Cozenza listening stared,
And marveled, silently, his changeful fate.
Concetta was the singer, whose sweet song
Etolia's startled thoughts remembered long :—
And this Concetta was so good and kind,
To sorrowing Etolia, that her mind
Had, like a flower beaten by the rain,
Lifted from drooping, its sweet bloom again.
Here need we tell the reader, that they met
Who late were parted with such keen regret ?
And soon the Cardinal, his ransom sent,
Would haste to Rome with direful, deep intent.
Against Salluzzi and his mountain band—
Forthwith exterminate them, from the land.

XV.

One day Salluzzi said: " I understand,
We have a little mystery on hand ;—
Those two, that lately met here, lovers are ;
And you, Capano, are the lucky star,
Resplendent o'er their fortunes, eh, my friend !
To marry them, and all their troubles end ?"
"Holy St. Francis," said his Eminence,
Alas! I feel departing my last sense
And ray of reason! No! I had decreed,
To take her with me, certainly, when freed :
She is a destined *clausura*, you know
For holy San Gregorio Armeno."

"No No! I think not," said Salluzzi, "try
What to all this, Etolia will reply."
And, strange as it may seem, whatever word
Faint and inaudible, Etolia heard,
In murmurs low, the day her mother died,—
She had on stern Salluzzi since relied—
No scorn or anger tinged her modest pride.
Etolia's tested heart, in trial just,
Some terrible avowal meekly made;
And questioned by the Cardinal, she must
Tell of Cozenza—yea; and though afraid,
Confessed the wish to wed that renegrade,
Except that she forbore repeating all
The titles giv'n him by the Cardinal.

XVI.

And they were wed in that deep, Sylvan dell—
No joyous herald or Cathedral bell;—
But hospitable was the mountain chief—
The tapers lighted, and the myrtle leaf
Twined for the festival, as though she were
His own beloved child so young and fair.
Her glossy hair, around the perfect head,
In braids entwined with pearl in many a strand—
Rubies, and emeralds, and diamonds laid
On scarlet velvet, for a zone whose band
Clasping her robe of satin pure and white—
O'er all a vail of lace, cast radiant light.

XVII.

And she was a bride; yet her soft tears fell:
She thought of the mother who loved her well—

Of the home so far in the mountain dell
Whose stately old halls were so silent now;
No echo had they of her low sweet vow :
In darkness the chambers where childhood played;
Now no festal garlands around them laid—
But Olive drooped shadow, and sun, and dew,
And the heavens of Neapolitan blue.

XVIII.

The peace of her sweet face, and happy heart,
Happy at last with him—no more to part—
No more to part? Alas! how few the days
Of tender gladness, like a bird's sweet song
That only dews and flowery woods prolong:
Or, where on morning's upward glory flung
The lark's wing joyous, till his matin sung,
Within the brown grass on the earth, he lays
A tired, silent breast of pain and praise.
The lime leaves, and the roses, and the air,
Thrilled with the holy presence—they were there :
They touched the silvery sands ; and soon the tide
Kissed them with veneration, as they hied
Forever hallowed to the deepest deep,
That sanctified, sweet memory to keep.
"Let me be with thee when our rescued altars,
All lighted, greet thine eyes to victory won ?
Nay ; like the sun robed sea, my heart ne'er falters,
From shore to deep, I am thy wave, O sun !"

XIX.

"It may not be, my love," Cozenza said;
"My country calls; and my sire's fallen head

Lifts from the sanguine dust a martyr's brow,
And looks upon the auspicious hour—now.
Now is the revolution close, and all
The sons of Sicily respond her call;
And when I bear thee to thy courtly home,
Thy liberator's name will risk its dome
'Tis true; but with success at last I'll come,
And triumph shall resound with trump and drum:
To this thy gentle thoughts may always tend
Through anxious waiting, dear, unto the end;
And keep thy quiet counsel, like the dove;
Content with loving, thou hast wed thy love;
But let none know it till the days have past
Of danger: haply, soon will be the last."

XX.

Beyond St. Elmo, the great mountain's crown—
Beyond the tomb of Virgil, nestled down—
That is—if doubt will spare its old renown;—
The road to Olevano from the town,
Beyond Martino Fidelissima
Whose inmates rarely speak—such is their law—
Princely and priestly and in history famed
For fierce rebellions, and now scarcely tamed;
But if, as we are told, that golden is
Silence, there is no need to mention this;—
But take their good example—keeping mum—
So much can be implied by seeming dumb;
Neither was Capri nor Ischia seen
From Olevano—the great mounts, between:[24]
But often on the balmy atmosphere

Vesuvius' curling smoke seemed rising near :
And now Etolia, in her Fathers' Halls,
Moved mid the birds, and bees, and waterfalls.

XXI.

Here a few radiant days, Cozenza stayed—
And then the parting that was long delayed;
The curved and grieving lip, with quivering thrill,
Fondly entreated as a woman will.
Her pleading, failing heart adjured him oft
With hand upon his arm, and upward soft,
Imploring glances. " Love, why stay not here !
Too much I love thee now—thou art too dear;
I do entreat thee it is not too late—
Compassion have on me, and heed thy fate ! .
Cozenza, in God's name, and by our love, [25]
What was the sequel when thy father strove ?
Oh to some desert fly ! and take me there,
Still blest with love and thee—no matter where."

XXII.

And true it was—all true—the things she told ;
And beautiful their home—that castle old,
With marble and fine stone in carvings scrolled.
To wander through its halls was like a dream
Wondrous with statues ; and the chastened gleam
Of treasured paintings every wall adorning;
The bannered ivy on the breeze of morning
Through the wide casements flowing darkly green;
And over keep and battlement, a screen
Of densely waving beauty—and the arch

Made circular—and pillars slenderly,
Like tall, cliff shadows on a sunset sea—
And old, armorial bearings of the march—
A semi-pointed delicate arcade—
The library and drawingroom—and laid
The ceilings and the staircases with gold
And silver ornaments of richest mold—
So beautiful this Roman castle old.
And many stories of the ages gone
It might have told—'twas older than Chillon.
Beside the warder's residence a tower,
And grassy courtyard bright with tree and flower
For now no gathering warriors mailed went forth
To burning Syria or the chilly north.
The gate doors heavily cased with iron plate
Were massive works of art strong and ornate:
On right hand from this entrance was a door
To chambers never used since days of yore;
Albiet for all domestic purpose fit
The portal was bricked up none nearing it:
But let us dare to enter, list and seek;
And to adjure its ancient ghosts to speak:
Dark emptiness and silence here recall
Some old dim record serving to appal,
Nothing is apparent—the Dining-hall,
And kitchen, and side rooms long vacant all—
Except a swinging bell whose dinner chime
Called the retainers in the olden time:
But ah! what other service did the bell—
Did the doomed prisoner note its clanging knell?
And why that moldy stircase of dark stone,

Leading to chambers darker yet and lone,
Downward beneath the Castle's whole right wing?
We shudder, and draw back—there is something
Weirdly absorbent in that stairs of gloom—
We turn away in awe as from a tomb.

XXIII.

Dear reader, say not that I have forgot
Etolia and Cozenza,—I have not:
I only lingered still, their parting o'er,
As they themselves did linger, and e'ermore
As lovers will who part and who adore.
Heavy, the anchors lift that leave the shore—
Each heart a treasure trove of memory
Never to come again from the deep sea.
Never again, Etolia, never again,
But then thou didst not know this dread sentence'
   pain.

XIV.

The last eve came. Within her chamber praying,
Etolia waited, her quick heart obeying
The sound of his approaching step. He came:—
The silence was a pang—at last her name ;—
Lowly and with a sob its utterance fell
From his proud lips, yea, from his deep heart's swell,
As when from Heaven the angel downward swept.
It seemed to come that little word. She wept;
And falling on her knees, she clung to him ;—
He covered his fond eyes so full and dim.
Ah! let them part; and let us not behold

Those few last moments—that entwining fold—
Until, from claspings close he rushed away—
Then, on her swooned eyes, still darkness lay:—
He knew not this, and hastening, did not stay.
At outer gate, his faithful followers stood
Waiting to guard his journey through the wood.
Glowing, the Milky-way's translucent path,
The splendid midnight of fair Naples hath;
But what to him, the light of shore or sea,
Whose thoughts were turbulent with memory:
The smoking summit, and the ruined streets
Of Pompeii, that near the traveler meets,
Were nought to him; his gloomy heart still turned
Back to Etolia: then would intervene,
Like meteors, through the darkness, brightly seen—
The patriot's bounding hopes—his blue Tyrrhene
Emblazoned, as with altar lights, it burned.

XXV.

The mounted cavalcade proceeded slow;
For changed the night to darkness, from the glow,
As dark as Erebus—the sheeted flame
Of lightning, on it momentarily came.
Hour after hour, they rode: at last, a small
Old hermitage they reached,—alighted all.
Before the door, a few fine shady trees—
This, the abode of hospitable peace—
An old man's home. After the weary mules
Were cared, and he had offered rustic stools,
And all his little store of figs and wine,—
He motioned to Cozenza with a sign

That in the room adjoining, there then lay
Three English travelers, who at dawn of day,
Would climb Vesuvius, that they might behold,
The sunrise of its glory,—red and gold—
But if there were some reason this was told,
I know not.   Then he gave a packet-fold
With much significance of silent look;
And gave for autographs, his "Travelers Book,"
As though the packet were Sisyphus' Stone,
And *he* Sisyphus, to its usage known—
The more—he lived upon the mount alone,
And these were strangers come, soon to be gone.

XXVI.

" Ah !"—said Cozenza to his comrade true,—
Caldara, whom, before my reader knew.
" *Che nuove* ?" asked the others, " Master,
Give us your orders, and we'll travel faster !"
"What news?" they asked again. He answered—
    " Brothers
'Tis true, we more must haste to join the others.
From Etna to the Alps, is every heart,
Ablaze with readiness to do its part :—
But well beware of Satriano's spies,
And let us leave here long before sunrise."
All this, in whispers, with directed eyes
To the partition of the other room.
"*Amice*—friends ! Close is the day of doom !
The royal troops advance Palermo's fate !—
The people fortify in haste, each gate !—
The towns and villages are burned along

The royal troops' red route of ghastly wrong !—
Five hundred of our men await me where
The mountain peasants gather,—we'll be there !
Not stronger burns Stromboli's riven heart
Than mine to meet them—let us now depart !"

CANTO SEVENTH.

The Commissario.

I.

Return to Olevano! The long days
Passed wearily; and oft Etolia's gaze
Would pierce the route he had departed by:—
The gray came into the November sky,
As turns the silvery white Maguolia leaf
From its first velvet balm so brightly brief.
How were the lonesome days of sadness spent?—
The Palace home was but an Arab's tent,
To her love-yearning heart that followed far,
Restless, she walked its colonnades, and leant
Over their casements—watched the vesper star
Until her eyes with tears would fill; and she
Would turn, and play some pensive melody.
Again, with purpose strong, upon the page
Of national proud annals, would engage
Her newly centered thoughts. Thus she could
　　learn
His favored authors all, ere his return,—

Botta, Santa Rosa,—and other books,
That for a decade, had not left their nooks, —
Great Macchiavelli, and Colletta,—
For books are good things to make one forget a
Heavy sorrow; or at least—to hide it—
Many a one, besides Etolia, tried it;
And many little tri-colors with skill
She worked, with secret smiles, at her own will,
To sée that sign on gold and silver lace,
On cushions, hangings, and on every space
In those proud, ancient halls of royal grace,
That blazed with courtly lineage gone before.
Some little thought, perhaps, it cost; but more
Cozenza was to her—"Love rules the Court,"—
She did not know our English version for't
But then, she felt it: and the camps, and groves
Of all her lineage, were not more than Love's.

II

At this time, Satriano's dread police
Had learned the secrets of this home of peace;
If any home of peace could then be found
In all of hapless Naples, terror crowned.
Aiossa and his Sbirro, fierce Bruno,
Silently, constantly, as shadows go,
Watched their unhappy victims doomed; and slow
The *Sedia ardente*, the warm chair,
Pontillo placed for them; and vain the prayer
Of wife, or son, or daughter, each might die;
Or, by confession, wrung from agony,
Betray the heroism, betray the life

Still dearer than their own. Such was the strife
And dread alternative to the fond wife
Of troubled days,—that, to his children dear,
The name of patriot father, though sincere,
Oft gave a double awe to love and fear.

III.

Turn to the page of record! We are told
Of iron rings of torture, made to hold
Limbs dislocated from the beauteous mold
Of the good Creator—extended arms
Turned in an instrument, which the base fiend
Luigi Maniscalco named; and screened,
Beneath his malice, mockery's alarms.
La Macchina Angelica 'twas called,
The deadly humor of the thing, appalled.
The old man, and the lovely woman who
Was with holy motherhood invested,
Suffered alike—if e'en suspicion threw
The name of patriot o'er them, they were tested.
There is a special mention made of two,
At Morreale, who were stripped, and beat
Till they expired at their tormentors' feet.

IV.

Neath thy cloud canopy, O Constantine!
The *Commissario's* cross,—black fatal sign;
And this, on Olevano's outer gate,
One morn was seen—portentous of its fate—
Under strict surveillance, this meant,—beware!
Etolia had received a letter, late

That very morn—so glad and grateful, there,
Thanking the God of journeyers, that *he*
Had safely reached his own bright Sicily—
Her husband! her adored and loving lord!—
And long she lingered, reading every word
Of his dear message:—and what secret, she
Would tell him joyous in its mystery—
What might she promise, his return should see.
Mater admirabilis! always thou,
A trembler in thy joy and love as now!

V.

But Hark! The heavy iron ball that swings
At Olevano's gate, against it rings!
Strangers, and clamorous with haste! again
Repeating the quick summons,—answered,—when
They asked for her! A party of three men—
They were a sort of Hydra altogether,
The Commissario, Morbili, rather.
Morbili! Heaven and Earth! that fearful name;
Condemned synonym, of the blackest blame.
As a scroll withers in remorseless flame ;—
As a frost falling, brings a flower blight:—
So, on Etolia their dread summons came ;
And yet she met them with a footstep light,
And bade them seated be, with easy grace:—
And firmly unperturbed, her lovely face.
Morbili and his spies—yes! there they sat ;—
Each one, a species of colossal rat;
Morbili's eyes were set, and looking at
A paper lying on the table near.—

" *Signora*, if you please, just hand that here !"
At this, Etolia's heart felt secret fear;
But there's a sort of courage giv'n the weak—
With dignity she rose—essayed to speak;
And gave the harmless paper he had asked,—
The precious and sweet letter in her breast
Was safe concealed; and, for the first time tasked,
She felt her fervid soul a battery masked,
Though outwardly, so calm in gracious rest.

VI.

Th'accuser's face was red, and round, and large ;
His voice pitched like the Boatswain's of a barge:
Another, sitting on the divan, read
The usual formula when making charge
Of conspiracy : some incipient dread
Had gathered all the servants round the door,
To listen while he read the charges o'er ;
And then with cries and lamentations, they
Gathered about their lady, like the spray
That round a white wave goes to share its shock
On the relentless and reboundless rock.
" As for these servants—let them all depart
Unto their several homes ; lest they too, share
The doom of treason's treacherous despair !"
Their desolation and her own did start
Upon Etolia's mind.—"Your power is strong;"
Proudly she said;—"their grief concerns me now,
You know that they are not accused of wrong !
Why then bring sorrow on a guiltless brow ?
You need not crush ! Your word is strong to spare !

And cannot some of them remain with me?"
"No! No! not one?" replied Duke Morbili.

VII.

Concetta Lavagna was weeping low,
And kneeling, gently clasped her mistress hand
Beside Etolia's chair.—Salluzzi's band,
Redeemed, all noble patriots of their land—
Had joined Cozenza, from their mountain Pass;—
And poor Concetta, also here—alas!
To share misfortune where she loving served—
Experience with danger, long had nerved
Her faithful heart, a heart that never swerved.

VIII.

With such urbanity as he could use,
The Duke informed Etolia, that she must
Regard herself—that is, should she refuse
To make what statements he considered just—
Under his authoritative arrest,
Unless her husband's plottings she confest.
He was a base insurgent, was he not?
Now gone to Sicily to organize,
Against the king, another secret plot—
But she might her own safety compromise
By giving information of his plans.
At this, the bright tears stood in her sweet eyes;
And sudden flushed her cheeks, then paled as sands,
The bright tide had bereft, and trembling some:
Morbili saw she was defiant,—dumb;—
More compliant, and with forbearing look

Or, a trite familiarity, he took
Concetta's hand; and lifting her, he said;—
"Weep not, my pretty one,—be not afraid!
In your case, I will say, you may remain;
And, on your aid, I will rely to gain
Your mistress over, from her perverse mood;
And, for this purpose, she shall have some days—
Meanwhile, a guard shall hold this rebel place—
Until I come again—'tis understood:—
Signora, one thing more,—the castle's plan
I have by me, avoid, as well you can,
The last appeal of justice.   I resort,—
(Here his eyes swiftly glanced across the Court.)
To the lone chambers long unoccupied,
And subtile horror his quick glance implied,
Meanwhile continuing with desperate haste,
As nervously his hand on hers he placed,
"'Tis true *Signora*; I resort, I said,
Only to measures stern, when others fail
No doubt, those dungeons old have many a tale
Of fruitless warnings and of sequels dread,
Of warnings terrible; but none so strange,
So inconsistent to all fitting things;—
I hope, *Signora*, that my meaning brings
Itself within the limit of your range
Of sensitive perception;—now adieu,
Signora," said the wretch, and then withdrew.

IX.

And soon the days passed; but in vain she tried,
Sad, faithful prisoner who on chance relied,

To find some messenger.   The servants all
Were searched with vigilance, and sent away,
Like wanderers, in the outside world, to stray;
For some of them, since childhood, in that Hall,
Had dwelt, and still in peace had hoped to dwell,
Changeless as those old halls, till life's closed day.
At first, Etolia thought,—"it is not well,
That I this trouble, to Cozenza tell:
Charged with so much of import as he is,
How can I hope the tyrant's blow to miss
Through his protecting arm ; my sorrow less
Will be, concealed from his so keen distress;
And even at the most, my sorrow's gloom
Must not precipitate my hero's doom,
Nor find weak refuge in my hero's tomb."

X.

The bright crusading banners were not stirred
By Syrian winds ; and on the thrilling eve,
The Harp and Paynim trumpet were not heard.
It was the Revolution's mighty heave—
Cowards in strongholds, well content to fire
Through the fair street, and o'er the splendid spire.
All the night long, upon the city fell,
The detonation of the bursting shell:
Vain was all watchful care,—the vandal deed
Struck in the household, childhood and old age;
Whoe'er had strength to fly, in flight's quick heed
Bereft the weak ; and love's power to assuage,
Could but, returning wild, rush in again,
To find a mangled child, or parent slain—

No roof secure ;—the stricken lambent flame,
From balcony and flowery casement came.
Around the walls, and sounding ancient shore.—
All day, all night, the cannon o'er and o'er,
Unceasing sent its dreadful, muffled roar.
Eight steamers came at midnight,—each a sting
From the great scorpion that some called their king;
Five thousand soldiers more, the bastioned gate
Of old Montaldo's faithful fires, did wait.
Fearful the conflict! vain, rampart and fort;
For step by step the people's fierce retort
Viva L' Italia! the last words to bless,
Of dying lips, still cheered dear bought success.
While from Montaldo rung the enfilade,
From house to house, through walls, the conflict
   made
Indomitable way ;—in ev'ry room, [26]
The bloody strife contested hand to hand :—
Let me not dwell upon the slaughter's gloom ;
For all of valor's feats, you understand,
Since it was old Palermo, brave and grand.

XI.

Out on the mountains, the following day,
To meet more entering troops upon their way ;
Hunger and thirst, through fierce long hours, they
   stood,
Their numbers, still like an increasing flood ;
Sending, at last, the messengers for food,
Entreating,— no bread came ; and then for water,
Resignedly, they asked, while still the slaughter

Reciprocal, endured until the eve,—
Alas! 'twas then discovered—and we grieve
To tell the Comitato's treason—they,
Withholding promised succor, did betray:—
A few hours more—victory to decide;
But vain the earnest hopes of those who tried;
Though faint with thirst and hunger, still they
    cried,
"Down with the Bourbon," and, like heroes, died:
And then a royal amnesty withdrew
From out the valliant ranks, a dastard few
Who weakly turned submissive and untrue.

XII.

On mount Calatifini, the Brigands
Managed their cannon with devoted hands—
Repentent and self sacrificing, who
Of all surpassed them, dauntless there and true—
Piled were the dead, Salluzzi dared not count,
Round the tricolor on that signal mount.
At last he sought Cozenza,—"Come remain
Not here," he said, "seek safety! All is vain!"
"Never!" Cozenza cried, "Behold the slain!
My hope was with them; and when now they meet
Reverse, with them shall be my last defeat!
I led them on to this,—*they* don't retreat!
Hungry, but victorious, here, this morn—
For treason and betrayal, see their scorn!"

XIII.

"Well, since you list not," said Salluzzi, " I
Will give you argument you can't deny,

Unless you would, like a sold traitor, die !
Suppose a sum were offered for your head,
Alive, or else to murder you instead—
General! your power and example have
Thwarted the enemy, aspired to savé
The country.   Knowing this, the traitors gave
A charge—you should not see another day.—
In these confused hours ;—in this hot fray
How easy, pulls a trigger,—and the sum
I might e'en name to you,—now will you come ?"
"None would accept it" said Cozenza; " Hold !
I have accepted it " Salluzzi bold
Replied, "and bargained for the deed in gold!
This will prevent all others from the dire
And dastard act—and now at once retire."

XIV.

" No! No!" Cozenza said, "thus saved attack,
To my brave fellows I will hasten back.
We'll wait here until dusk—thereafter, soon
The signal lights will rise—late shows the moon ;
And then, Salluzzi, watchful care and chance
Must see the men all ready for advance.
Surprise the garrison, *Palazzo di Finanze;*—
One hundred men from Borgo and Colli,
Commanded by Suchelli, will set free
The prisoners ; if failure meet their aim,
Their faithful service will be judged the same,
To keep the troops of Molo all the night,
Engaged, someway, in desultory fight,
And I, at Porta d'Ossone, will stand—

You know the mansion quarters, near at hand,
And thence, myself, go on to the attack
Upon Noviziato;—you'll be back—
More victory and success, we'll meet to tell—
If not, then *Camerata*—now, farewell!"

XV.

Again, to Olevano's let us go
And see what more, its storied days may show
The next time that Morbili came, he brought [27]
Bruno and Pontillo, who first had wrought
The torture beams similar to a rack:
Another, too, accompanied them back—
Her friend, the Cardinal, to comfort her,
And to advise her obstinate self-will.
She was not corteous—for she did not stir
When his name was announced; but sitting still,
She seemed to nerve herself anew.   He came
With fatherly regard, apparently;
And took her hand, and softly called her name.
"My daughter!" then he said, "what fearful blame
Is this which lieth heavily on thee?
And will you not confess it all to me?"

XVI.

"Father, you know I cannot hope to win
Your favor—for, at first, you called it sin."
"And so I did, my child—this undenied;—
Commit not sacrilege with it beside,
Disloyal to your King—of this accused."
Etolia, faintly smiling, then perused

His face, with meaning looks, and gently said;
"You *know I'm loyal* to *my* king, instead;
But as for *your* king,—I scarce understand;
Though I suppose that *you* mean Ferdinand."
He smiled in turn; her meaning he perceived:
Too late, he looked sincerely, deeply grieved;
And told her earnestly, he could not save
Her direst consequence, unless she gave
Account explicit of all secret plot.
Vain, was her strict assurance, she had not
The knowledge asked her: "They would not
  believe,"
He answered sternly;—"nor could he retrieve
The suff'ring she would bring upon herself,
Ending, no doubt; and honored with a shelf
In the old vaults her ancesters long filled—
And some of them, like her, had been self-willed."

XVII.

Here poor Etolia looked at him, and thrilled
With trouble and foreboding. Quickly flew,
As unto heavy flowers their full dew,
The tears into her gentle eyes of pain.
He could not bear this; and he said again ;—
"Think of what I advise; and let me find,
On my return, such change of heart and mind,
As will, my child, restore all gracious trust
With our good Ferdinand, so great and just."
"Your Eminence, I will not change one inch ;
And persecution will not make me flinch:
Too well I've learned the very doctrines you

Inculcate nobly—ever to be true
To my dear Lord, even should martyrdom
From ev'ry deathly horror on me come;
And now farewell! I cannot bear suspense."
Again her fine lip's curve grew close and tense,
As though made ready to endure all things:
Her friend departed amid whisperings
And anxious looks, that followed, of the Guard
Gathered in Olevano's old court-yard.

XVIII.

Three days elapsed; and then the Order was,
To have her up for trial formally—
The Charge repeated, of offended laws—
If so desired, she might send for, and see
Her husband or her friends—O, mockery!

XIX.

In the lone chambers that had long been closed,
Morbili's Court held session; and there sat
Pontillo, Del Caretto; and there dozed
Old Cardinal Capano, just as fat
As ever, though, 'tis true, he fretted at
Etolia's strange perversity; but sin
Had not the evil power to make him thin:
As for Etolia, she had lately grown
Like a swooned lily by a storm-wind blown.
When called, she answered; and she told her name,
Her station, and her lineage, whence she came.
At this, Capano waked, and wiped his eyes,
Grief had o'ercome him, or sleep, or surprise:

Reproaching her, he left her to her fate;
But, secretly, himself, he blamed—too late:
Too late, he had advised;—too late, he sought
Her youthful, wayward counsel ; and just brought
The culmination he could not avert:
The stern old fellow felt a little hurt,
And more alarmed—but tried to justify
Himself—she could control her destiny,
If she were not so perverse, and of mood
Intractable—not easy understood.
Thus angered and distressed, he could not stay ,
And ere the trial closed, he drove away.

XX.

Etolia was remanded, till once more
She should be called.   Wearily at the door
Of her sad chamber, entering she met
Concetta weeping.   "Lady, you forget
What record awful, and alone I keep,
Some day, account to render !   Why not weep ?
"Twere better I were dead, than live to tell
To Count Cozenza, of what things befell
My Lady, were she dead from torture's pain,
Or those o'erwhelming troubles that obtain
Ascendancy.   What would they ask ?—tell all !
Your telling it, will not make aught befall
The Count Cozenza—he is safely far—
A fearless destiny, his ruling star—
Shielded by faithful hands of love, and hearts;—
Each, a defender, at his danger starts."

XXI.

And thus the good Concetta, vainly tried
Propitiation that was still denied
Gently but firmly. "No, Concetta, friend!
Your unremitting care may too soon end;
Go to Palermo, with your trust sincere,
And find him, if you can, whom I hold dear;
And tell him—ah great God! alas! I fear
The death of battles in his brave career,—
You will not e'er have need—he may not hear:
Firm still thy fortitude, as fondly brave,— .
At least, Concetta, try thyself to save:
Go quickly when they free thee, which they will—
But tell him nothing hastily, until
Surmises of these things first come, as on
The sunset cometh night, ere 'tis begun:
You know, Concetta, not to give him pain
Sudden or terrible, but to refrain,
And wait his stricken evidence of woe:—
Have you not watched the creeping tidal-flow,
The overwhelming and relentless main,
So like to agony's slow, boundless throe
That cannot be restrained?—No, No! ah no!—
Concetta, tell him thus—let fall the blow
Lightly as possible—you know—you know!"

XXII.

Her voice was hushed! She did not speak again:
That day, they fastened a light, strong, steel chain
Around her beauteous arm:—the castle rung
With hammer blows: a ring, in which was hung

The chain, was driven in the wall; and swung
The width of her apartment—and no more:
She now was prisoner close within its door;
And of Concetta's constant care—forlorn,
She waked to miss e'en that the coming morn.
Her only food was now a little bread,
Having refused Capano's further aid,
Which gave her judges reason to believe
Her contumacy meant but to deceive
With vague, evasive answers for the truth:
—They had no pity on her love or youth.

XXIII.

After the first dread trial, when remanded,
She seemed a fragile wreck, storm-washed and
    stranded.
She thus was kept, a few days in her room—
The cruel chain still adding to her gloom;
But firmly patient, her calm apathy
Had almost overcome anxiety ;
The seals were broken on her founts of hope;
The sunlight, and the verdure from the slope
Had vanished; and, relying but on God,
Already, the dark valley's path, she trod :
Pressed deeply in by death and girdling grief,
She only prayed, their agony be brief.
Once more Morbili questioned her, and took
Occasion, holding judgment, to rebuke
Her reckless disregard of her own fate;
In many pompous words, assumed to state
The nature of the punishments—when he

Lost further patience with obstinacy.
Vain was her terror—vain his every threat;
Morbili was so angry that he roared:
She almost heard the sound of her heart's beat;
But seemed, above all terror, to have soared.

XXIV.

"Take her," he said; "and let her then be thrown
Into the dungeon, though she die alone!"—
Even the guards could scarce suppress a groan,
Hearing this sentence. When the court adjourned,
She was not to her lonely room returned:
Drear as it was, it had both light and air;
But these had vanished when below the stair
Of cold, gray stone, that to the dungeons led,
Where she was taken, less alive than dead:
And still her food—hard bread—a little water;
Incredible, yet true; that nurtured daughter
Of delicate fine race, imprisoned lay,
Perishing by want—hid from light of day.
Martyr of Justice! even this,—and lo!
There is more yet to tell,—thy final woe!

XXV.

Next day, the Order was to take her up:
Morbili feared she'd die, before the cup
Of bitterness was drained to its last drop.
"Where is she?" said the seeking men: "Just stop
We'll call her, for 'tis dark as Hades here!
She may be hid, or sleeping somewhere near."
They called; and nothing answered, save the sound

Reverberate of their voices,—all profound
Dark stillness, through the damp, deep dungeons,
   round.
His minions sought her in the *barathrum*,[28]
A pit below the floor—the Tullianum
Of Rome was the original of these—
Old prisons, or old cesspools, as you please,
For sometimes they conjoined the common sewer;
And those cast in, were never heard of more.

XXVI.

In one such horrible and Orcus place—
Still groping, and still finding not a trace
Of her whom there they left, the night before—
With careful hands, they touched the walls, the
   floor :
At last—" I see her," said one of the men,
"There she is crouching in a bunch, I think !
I guess she's not quite healthy in this den !
Perhaps, she's fainted, and should have a drink,
Or needs some one to fan her ; the rose cloud
Of her soft cushion is not here allowed ;
And she is sulky, is she not ?" Each jest,
While she was all unconscious of their quest,
Heartless and ghastly passed o'er her deep rest;
For those were demons of Morbili's own,
Used to such scenes—rare jewels of the Crown.

XXVII

They moved her, finding her so quiet; and,
When lifted up, they saw she could not stand :
They carried her, and laid her down outside:

The firm white lips were closed : the gentle pride
Of her deep, lovely eyes, was lidded down,
But softly quivered when the pure air, blown
Upon her face, revived her; and she sighed:
And soon she murmured, "Light, so strange ! so
    still !
So beautiful ! What sounds, the sweet air, fill ?
Again I breathe ! My God ! have I not died ?"
—As human nature varies kind good will
For scorn's indifference to outside things—
No more compassion's sympathetic thrill
Alleviated her great sufferings :
None to behold them, whom affection moved;
The very guards who had, at first, so proved
Their deep remonstrance by, at least, a groan,
Had into use been hardened—horror gone;
And gentle, mild respect had even flown.

XXVIII.

For now, so weary and so faded, weeks   .
Of woe had made her—she seemed not the same.
Upon the fairest, harrowing care soon wreaks
His blows of iron; and her fragile frame
Bore evidence of this.   Pontillo came—
" You may be executed," he observed,
" If, for endurance, you are not well nerved :
—You may, it so desired, bind up your brow :
It has become severest duty now,
Signora, to extort confession—sit
On the *ardente sedia*, and fit
This iron band about your temples, please;

Or I will have it done, if you permit,—
I cannot help it,,if you feel it squeeze—
And hasten; there's no use in such long prayer."
—Absorbed, and answ'ring not, Etolia there
Was lowly kneeling; "Lord, my God ! to thee,
I offer up my life submissively !
Save him for whom I die, since upon me
Hath come the sacrifice ! Cozenza! Love!—
Perfect the struggle that my death will prove."

. XXIX.

They seized, and placed her in the *Burning-chair:*
Her raiment that had been so light and fine,
Grew slowly scorched ; and on her temples fair,
The iron band's slow. tight'ning, dented line
Bled, and she moaned : then Pontillo cried,
    "There !
Take her outside, and let her have some air !"
They watched her for some sign's returning life—
But vainly—she was freed from further strife.
Stretched on the earth, her pale pure brow, marked
    round
With the blue, bleeding line, the iron bound :
In vain they dashed cold water on her face :—
She stirred not from her finished, quiet grace !
In peace, Etolia! to thy resting place
Go now, sweet soul, for all is consummated !
And better to have died unconscious thus,
Than to have lived to learn, what life still fated—
More grievous to thy heart, than life's own loss.

CANTO EIGHTH.

Castell' a Mare.

I.

Remember where Cozenza and Salluzzi stood
Together, near Headquarters, in the mountain-
wood;
All was disaster that eventful night—
Betrayal, panic, death, and wounded flight.
A tramping patrol found our hero, laid
Near *Porta di termina*—some dismayed
Adherents, hopeless, fled, and left him there:
He was unconscious, bleeding; but with care—
The patrols knew their prisoner—what rare
Captive they carried to *Castell' a mare.*
He wakened, wounded unto death almost;
And many days and weeks in fever, tossed:
His heart beat, and his nerves with grieving thought:
He felt, to execution, he'd be brought;
All outside freedom he had left behind;
But civilly, the captain had consigned
Him to an officer on duty—he
Was kept a prisoner, but yet was free

To walk at leisure.   When he stepped inside,
He saw the bridges drawn that then denied
Him egress from that place; and he felt sure
There was no life for him beyond its door.

II

Along the ramparts, up and down, he walked;
And careless with the guards, unnoticed talked:
One day, at change of sentinels, he passed
The square where piles of guns and shells were
    massed
In pyramidal rows—a martial kind
Of armament: pond'ring, he thought to find
The means of some escape: absorbed, he rose
With equal hope to projects; but all those,
Each after each, appeared impossible.
At last, as chance would have it, so it fell,
That, unintentionally, he ascended,
And reached the line made circular that ended
The rampart of the bastion by the sea :
At ev'ry fort he crossed, he cordially
Returned the call, and said;—" Your Captain's
    guest !"
The guards were newly mounted, but had known
The kindness that their officer had shown
This prisoner—their minds were quite at rest.

III.

Continuing his tour along the left,
He saw the windows of the Chapel where
The prisoners, condemned,—of hope bereft,—
Passed three days, previous to their last, in prayer,

Or any other way the notion took them—
'Twas just an incubus contrived, that shook them
With cruel horror till their day of doom,
Slowly and coldly, in that chapel's gloom.
He shuddered. and passed on; and soon he found
A sentinel who talked much, on his round,
About the weather, and the soldiers' lives—
In fact, the whole line of his genealogy,—
And would have gone to Solomon and his wives,
Without the least remorse, or an apology,
But for an incident that then occurred,
And drew attention without further word :
A woman, holding on her arm a basket
Containing cakes and bottles, crying out
" *Biscata, Zembu !*"—Though she did not ask it,
She seemed to claim attention: she was stout,—
And was, perhaps, disguised :—with this impressed,
Cozenza watched her, and when near, addressed :

IV.

" *Signora*, will you bring a flask of wine
Or a good cake ?" Instinctively, a sign,
As of some motion or ulterior aim,
She made: he started—sure, she was the same,
His friend Concetta, whom he thought so far—
Perplexity and fear made quickly war
Within his anxious mind ; he dared not speak :
She noted soon the pallor on his cheek;
And swiftly spoke, herself—lest he might say,
Incautiously, some word that would betray—
" If you will wait ten minutes," answered she,

Resuming where he stopped; recovering, he,
Prompted instinctively, then quickly drew
Five pieces from his pocket; ere she knew,
He placed them with strong pressure in her hand :
—Though both were silent, did she understand ?

V.

She left him musing; and his restless mind
Waved like a night-bird in a stormy wind:
He sighed, and almost cursed his luckless fate
When struck the hour, a-quarter-past-of-eight.
Fainter, the sentinels, each after each,
Answered, *Allerta sta,* along the line:—
Beneath him stretched the sea, night's dismal reach;
But action, and not musing, must prolong
His life now menaced by oppression's wrong.
Of the late incident, what meant the sign
Concetta gave him ; and why was she here ?—
Again his heart thrilled with some startling fear;
Again appalling truth flashed on him—chance
Alone could save him—as a poising lance,
His purpose on the soldier he resumed:
To humor him awhile, his words were plumed.

VI.

Ere long the woman reappeared, and placed
A bottle and two tin cups on the ground;
And stood in such a manner, that she faced
Cozenza.   Hurriedly, she glanced around;
And then, intently at him, and retired.
His very heart was striking ; he respired
With hard-won effort; each breath seemed a knell;

He dared not ask her aught; she dared not tell:
—All these surmises and transpired affairs,
Were a few moments; thus, when danger stares,
We feel and think intently, in a space
Much shorter than in any other case.

VII.

Cozenza, then, with forced light jollity,
Said; "*Camerata*, what say you, if we
Drink the king's health?" "You know I cannot—
    thanks,
Signor! drinking on duty, and such pranks,
Place us upon retirement in the tanks!"
"Come" said Cozenza; "I'm your Captain's guest!"
—This "reasonable" reason seemed the best—
Forthwith, this genial comrade of the ranks
Ignored such small offence of dicipline:
He thought not twice, but took the little tin;
Cozenza took the other, filled it up—
"Here's the king's health!" he said, in whispered
    tone ;
Then deftly down his shirt front, it was thrown.
The soldier drank, at once, the tempting cup—
"Excellent!" he smacked. "Take another chum,"
Cozenza graciously repeated; "Come!"

VIII.

Again he filled it, and the bottle tost
Over the rampart to the seething sea—
Of all the many things of time, long lost—
Not the least costly of its argosy:

A moment more, the soldier heavily
Began to stammer; soon he sank and slept.
To the aperture of the cannon, crept
Cozenza softly : as he looked below—
There were the rocks—the sea in turbid flow:
If, he should throw himself—the certain risk—
'Twas thirty feet beneath the Cannon's disk.
The massive rocks that, piled against the wall,
Kept off the breakers, would receive his fall:
To shudder was to fail; the cups he threw
Into the Ocean, and his pistols too.
The night was pitchy dark, of blackest hue:
Heaven and Earth seemed joined in one dense mass:
The troubled waters sounded with the pass
Of strong harmonious winds. The tower's bell
Struck the last quarter—cold his heart's blood fell,
Then came the cry from the first sentinel,
And answered through the line, the "All is well!"

IX.

But here, one guard lay senseless, at his feet,
Who should respond to make the line complete—
Discovery, imminent—the moments, fleet.
Again the Sentry's voice—continuing,
The next to him should call it; and thus bring
The repetition to his post:—the string
Of his large cloak he held, to gather close
The two ends in his hands, before he'd spring:
He lingered; one more effort—heard the call,
And answered—then he leaped the bastioned wall.

X.

Swift as an arrow shot from bended bow,
He disappeared upon the rocks below—
No sound came from the turbid, onward flow.
Great Heavens! who shall ask the dark repose
Was then his quivering form in death's last throes?
Or was he swept out on the tide's high swell,
The requiem of the deep his only knell;
He had commended to the God of woes,
His reckless spirit; and not yet did close
That passionate, strong life: his form arose
Above the dark abyss—survived the leap—
Some other awful destiny to keep.

XI.

His ample cloak, wide floating on the wind,
Seemed as a spirit of the gloom, consigned
To the deep halls of Neptune, there to find
Repose denied on Earth to all mankind:
—'Twas not that of Elias,—nor the wing
Of the old Roman Eagle, fluttering;
But 'twas more adequate, if anything—
For upward it sustained him in his fall,
As mostly, our own cloaks do, after all.

XII.

He fell upon the rocks, and seemed unharmed;
Though stunned a little, groping as one blind,
He almost felt as if his life were charmed:
Escaped he was; and nothing heard behind—
The castle all was silent—unalarmed;—

Then with redoubled courage, plunged to cross
The basin small, between him and the land.
Forward in struggle with the waves' high heave,
Half vainly, did the desperate swimmer toss:
The water reached his chin, and ev'ry wave
Smote like a thunderbolt against his hand;
And o'er his head, with mighty roar, it fell
Upon the beach's smooth, extending swell.

XIII.

At last, he reached the shore; the boats were all
Drawn up, and formed a crest, or coronal:
His foot scarce rested on the land, when he
Turned back his gaze appalled, upon the sea;—
The rocks he had escaped; the Tower from whence
He leaped;—but lo! what dimness closed his sense:
His wounds were bleeding fresh : he felt the warm,
Life-blood fast oozing from his breast, and arm:
He dared not rest there, lest alone he'd lie
Unconscious all the night, or lonely die.
He dared not enter, through *Porta Felice*,
The city, lest he meet the dread Police.
Then, to the mountains he must go, though long
The road and, met at every turn, a throng
Of patrols: yet with cautious care he might
Hope to escape their notice, in the night.
Wearily on, some distance, toiled he slow,
Striving to justify his present woe;
Better it were to die, if die he must,
In proud defiance—for his cause so just,
Such death were not defeat—lonely but free,

And not the victim of ignominy.

XIV.

Ah! can we think of him in that dread hour?
He was going to die—each failing power
Left him with sinking faintness of the heart;
The long road silent, made each light sound start
His quiv'ring nerves, and o'erwrought trembling
  frame:
Each moment, he expected but to hear
The Castle's loud alarm, rung far and near.
—Still on he walked, or struggled till he came
To a dense grove of Olives; there he lay,
Not much unlike *One* of an ancient day:
He thought he rested; but a deathly faint
Came over him.—Farewell, Cozenza, now!
Thy white face upward looked—a soldier saint!
The chilly dews were on thy glorious brow!
Dying alone, with none to aid, or know—
Not all alone: there was a form came near,
So light her footstep that he scarce could hear.

XV.

This was the battle spot of recent strife,
Vanquished with sacrifice and yielded life;
And here, Love sought the Dead,—Lavagna's wife
Sought Lavagna; affection, more than fear—
Where wild dogs feasted; and were coldly strewn,
Unburried, half the dead, beneath the moon.
Dimly in death, Cozenza scarce could see
Concetta. Did she know him? Bending close—
*8

'Twas not the one she sought mid death's repose—
But 'twas Cozenza; and she started back ;
—A cloud passed o'er the moon, and made it black.
"He dies," she said, "now he need never know."
Kneeling, she held his hand, and raised his brow,
And listened to the words he murmured low,
For he had rallied : he was finely strong,
And highly wrought, with effort ; and ere long,
From his cold, paling lips there came a name—
To Love, and Life, and Death—it was the same.

XVI.

"My own Etolia! named for happy skies!
The anguish of the dying on me lies!
Oh, for one look of thy adoring eyes!
Then, as the brave from combats, would I go,
Thy pride and tenderness surmounting woe!
Farewell, Etolia, my Beloved! Farewell!
Upon the waters, sank the crimson, swell
Of the last sunset I shall e'er behold!
Our bugles silent; and our banners' gold,
Furling and folding in the purple gloom
Of the far distant mountains—fitting tomb
For noble efforts vain.   O wife! to-night,
The face thou lovest, will be cold and white!
Around me are the dead, on altar rocks—
Devoted hearts and brave, forever quenched—
Their true and tried hands on their musket-locks,
Or on their broken bayonets, coldly clenched.
And when thy chains are falling, fair, dear land!
Long will have perished, my love-daring hand!

Once more, farewell, sweet wife! sweet Love of
   mine!
To thee and to my God, my soul I sign,
Red, with the Martyr's signet! Oh, thy tears
I feel; and thy soft voice falls on my ears
Like waters in Cascades whose music fills
Th' embosomed beauty of our native hills!—
My heart's thrill, fainter grows! Take my last
   breath—
Etolia and Italia! Love and Death!"

XVII.

Unsanctified? No, No! yet he is dead!
Vainly, yet so loved—the oppressor's foe!
The transport of his radiant cheek is fled,
—As a wave's ripple, as a star's soft glow.
Submerged to gleam beyond, to shine below—
Along the glittering water's distant flow,
When the enchanting clouds, disparting, blow—
So lived, and died this one! the glorious brave!
His own blue Tyrrhene skies are o'er his grave;
And Myrtle blooms, and Olive o'er it wave.
O land! whose lava streams poured out, turn cold—
Still, from thy burning mounts, those streams are
   rolled!

XVIII.

Feronia, Goddess bright! thy sacred woods [29]
Shade not *Soracte;* but thy holy floods
Pour downward to the sea; —no votaries' hands,
And faces fair now wash upon their sands:

For thee, 'twas said, the feet bare palmed, could
   go
Across the burning coals, though burning slow,
Without the senses' pain of human woe.
Fides! the oaths of honesty were kept [30]
For thee, for whom first incense Numa swept :
But what of all this sacrifice of old ?
Italia ! are thy heroes now less bold?
The water now is blood—she sylvan chalice, gold !
Thy wings are upward, and with love sublime,
Thy martyrs hung their crowns on towers of Time,
Expiring for thy glorious destiny—
Upon their lips, assurance thus to thee,
ITALIA ! RISE EXULTANT, AND BE FREE !

FAMA SEMPER VIVAT.

L'ENVOY.

Reader ! if patient toil have brought
To thee, in verse, one pleasing thought;
Or thrilled within thy fervent breast,
One hidden chord from deep unrest
  Of sacred love's sweet pain—
Then shall the task, to me assigned,
Repay my weariness of mind;
And, ere we part—a short farewell,—
I seem to hear thy kind lips tell
  Of efforts not in vain.

Take from Pactolus' sands the little gold,
Take the bruised frankincense from desert lands;
O'er all the rest time's ocean shall be rolled—
How well I know, thy heart, this understands.

Bound with torments like waters of Sophene,
Bounded with waters of some blank despair,
Till death's strong trident from their shadows lean
To strike the lips that have no further prayer.

The shine of marbles in the summer sun,
The sway of grass upon the sunshine breeze;
This, the cold glory of the fair things done,
And the deep cadence of their after peace.

NOTES.

NOTE 1.—PAGE 20.

At Cannæ, whose historic plain.

The scene of this terrible battle was the plain, between Cannæ
and Anfidus, which was anciently called Campi Diomedis. Here
the consuls, Æmylius and Varro, made a desperate and futile resistance to the implacable conqueror Hannibal, on the 21st of May
216 B. C.

NOTE 2.—PAGE 21.

Along Voltorno's vale, the rain.

The valley of Voltorno takes its name from Vulturnus, a river of
Campania, rising in the Appenines, and falling into the Tyrrhene
Sea, after passing Capua. The Romans, at the battle of Cannae,
suffered additional disasters from the destructive wind which blew
from the side of the Vulturnus.

The valley is noted for its luxuriant fruitfulness; although its
cities, towns, and marks of ancient splendor, have nearly passed
away.

NOTE 3.—PAGE 21.

Gaeta only lives in name;

The town of Gaeta is distant 41 miles north-west from Naples,
and 72 miles south-east from Rome.

This town owes its foundation to the Læstrigones, and its name
to the nurse of Æneas, according to Virgil.

At this spot, around the famed Hill of Formæ, the Læstrigones
made their first settlement, on arriving from their fabled Sicilian
dominions. Homer mentions Lamus as their Capitol, which was
also tne name of their leader. The Cathedral of Gaeta contains
some curious and antique relics, one of which is the Vase in the
Baptistery, a singular specimen of antiquity. There is also a celebrated column with twelve faces, on which are engraved the names
of the different points of the compass, in Greek and Latin.

Between Mola and Gaeta are the ruins of Cicero's supposed Villa which he called the Formianum, a name derived from Formiæ the Hill above mentioned, the more ancient name of Gaeta. In its immediate vicinity, Cicero was put to death by an edict of the Roman triumvirate.

·NOTE 4.—PAGE 21.

Him who would gain Capua's gates;

About a mile beyond the present town of Capua, are the ruins of the ancient and celebrated Capua, once the chief city of Campania, of Etruscan origin.

Its first founders called it Vulturnus, by which name they designated the river upon which it stood. Its change of name was effected by the Samnite conquerors. Here Hannibal made his residence, after his great victory at Cannæ. On his departure, the Romans visited their displeasure upon the place for having made him welcome; and nearly reduced the city and the adjacent country to a desert.

At the time of Julius Cæsar, the Senate thought of restoring it. From this time it began to recover its former magnificence and flourished till it fell, with the rest of the falling empire, on the invasion of the barbarians. It contained at one time, about 800,000 inhabitants; and its vast amphitheater could entertain 100,000 spectators. This city was once so opulent that it even rivaled Rome, and was called *altera Roma.*

The most remarkable remains of its buildings, are the ruins of an amphitheater, of a subterranean gallery, and of a triumphal arch.

On the spot where it stood, has been built the town of *Santa Maria*, remarkable for its royal chateau which is one of the most magnificent in Europe, known as the palace of Caserte, whose architect was Vanvitelli; it cost seven million ducats.

The modern town of Capua is noted for its Cathedral which contains some columns of granite taken from ancient buildings, some good pictures, and various sculptures by Bernini. The church of the Annonciade merits observation; and under the piazza of the Place des Juges, are several antique inscriptions; on digging the foundations of the acqueduct for the above palace of Caserte, an ancient tomb was discovered 90 feet below the surface, and supposed to be 2000 years old.

NOTE 5.—PAGE 22.

Antony's mandate was fulfilled.

The enmity which Cicero bore to Antony was fatal to him. During the triumvirate of Augustus, Antony, and Lepidus, the name of Cicero was found upon Antony's list of proscription. The emissaries of Antony pursued Cicero to his home near Gaeta.

Among them was Popilius whom Cicero had once defended upon an accusation of parricide.

Cicero had fled towards the sea; and when the assassins came up to him, he put his head out of the litter, and it was severed from his body, by Herennius.

This event happened in December, 43 B. C., in the 64th year of his age. The head, and right hand of the orator, were carried to Rome, and hung up in the forum. Cicero was not only the first orator, but he was, unquestionably, the most learned philosopher of Rome.

Note 6.—Page 22.

If thou Campagna, drear and lone !

The desolation of the Roman Campagna is most oppressive. The stations, between the sea and the "Eternal City," are eleven in number; and nothing can surpass their lonely appearance. They are, simply, little round hovels at alternate distances—each surmounted by a wooden cross, imparting to it and the surrounding landscape a tomb-like character of utter desolation.

A few tired and demure ponies, and a stray shepherd or two, break the monotony of the view.

While the traveler may imagine his train drawn by oxen—so slowly does it advance over the buried ruins of antiquity, and past the startled buffaloes .that depart at its approach—the ferocity of Sylla, and the stealth of Cataline are, perhaps, the only harmless suggestions, to fancy, that are left; and with the last rays of the setting sun streaming their mellow light on the Campagna, "one may arise from his seat, in reverence to departed greatness," while entering the gates of Eternal Rome.

Note 7.—Page 22.

If, from the Aventine's crushed dome,

The Aventine, though not the largest of the seven hills of Rome, had upon it many important temples and many consecrated altars. The temples of Diana, Flora, Juno, and others, were on the Aventine.

The sites of some of them, so numerous and ancient were they, are now questions of remote uncertainty. The precise spot, where stood the temple of Liberty, is not now known. The *Bona Dea* is supposed to have stood on the site, afterwards chosen by the knights of *Malta* for their church, *St. Maria Aventina*.

There were, also, a temple of Minerva, and the sepulchre of Tatius into whose hands the gates of the city were betrayed by Tarpeia. Here was the cave of Cacus, the robber : the identity of this retreat has become a question of debate as to which side of the

Hill it honored, and must be left to share the fabulous and classical antiquity of the altars of Evander and Laverna. Cacus was the terror of Italy until strangled by Hercules, some of whose cows, Cacus had stolen and dragged into his cave. But the spot on which Hercules erected an altar to Jupiter Servetor in honor of his victory over the robber who while vomiting fire and smoke held a brave contest with his adversary, and the spot into which the cows were dragged, are places of equal, anxious inquiry, and classic commentary by the historian of to-day. Other antiquities, connected with this Hill, are the altar of Jupiter Elicius, the fountain of Picus and Famus, and especially the temple of Juno Regina built and consecrated by Camillus after the capture of Veii.

NOTE 8.—PAGE 23.

So thou, fair Cumæan Sibyl!

The Cumæan Sibyl seems to have been endowed with as many names as some of our modern writers. She is known by the numerous and respective appellations of Amalthæa, Daphne, Manto, Phemonoe, Deiphobe, Herophile and Demophile—she may have possessed the latter name in consequence of a suggestive analogy now obscurely veiled in the records of Mythology. It is said that she was seven hundred years old when Æneas came to Italy, and was still doomed to live as many years as she had grains of sand in the palm of her hand. She was endowed with the length of days by some mysterious favor of Appollo who loved her, and sought in vain from her a response to his passion. The doom of her refusal was that the years, though given to her, did not reserve to her the bloom and beauty of her lovable days. She pined in melancholy; paleness and despondency succeeded cheerfulness and youthful gaiety. She in turn destroyed two thirds of her own writings, because Tarquin the second refused to accept them. When she offered him the three remaining books, which at first had been nine in number, he accepted them, regretting the loss of the others, and cherishing those that remained with the greatest care. They were called the Sibylline verses; and so great was the reverence of the Romans for those prophetic books, that a college of priests was appointed to have the special care of them.

The fate of the Sibylline books is not actually known, They are supposed to have been burned in some of the great conflagrations, of which, I have mentioned the Alexandrian Library as being the greatest. Some of those under mention may have been saved, and collected after the burning of the Capitol, but this is not assuredly known—for, the books now extant called the Sibylline verses are *eight* in number, and treat of much pertaining to the history of Christ's Passion and the events of the christian era; for this reason they are thought to be subsequent to the original, and therefore

spurious—they are, however, full of sublime beauty, and surpass,
at least, equal the predictions and descriptions of *Isaiah*; and are
supposed to have been written as *Sibylline* in order to influence the
judgments of pagans in the first christian efforts at conversion.
The cavern of the Sibyl consisted of one vast chamber hewn out of
the solid rock. It was dedicated as a temple of Apollo, and was
almost entirely destroyed in a siege which the fortress of Camæ,
then in possession of the Goths, maintained against Narses.
" Maiden of Cumæ! Virgin, like Iphigenia, immolated for kings!
Thou didst receive the kiss of Apollo upon thy lips, the shadow of
the laurel on thy brow, the immortality of genius in thy bosom!
Thou wert formed to intone a song of harmony which should vibrate
through countless ages!"

NOTE 9.—PAGE 23.

"For relics of the proud Clev"

The efforts of England and the United States, to rescue from
silent destruction, the Egyptian obelisks, are so recent, that they
require but little mention ; However we may regret the removal of
those ancient monuments of art from their centurial places of
native repose, it is a matter of supreme relief to all lovers of antiquity, that Cleopatra's needle was safely rescued from impending
loss at sea, during the comparatively recent transportation of the
one taken to England, from the shores of Alexandria. The modern
world is perhaps justified in this preservation or desecration since it
is probable that one at least, of the needles of Cleopatra, would
eventually have become buried in the sands of Egypt. More than
forty years ago Cummings found one only of them stood in Hiero-
glyphic and lonely grandeur;—an elegant single block of granite,
seven feet square, and fifty in height;—the other lay prostrate and
already half burried in the sand of Egyptian Time.

NOTE 10.—PAGE 26.

Deserted Pisa ! long each towering dome

The Pisa of to-day is truly called" Deserted Pisa !" although
her monuments are carefully preserved and renovated by modern
art. The solitude is impressive, despite the brightness of Italian
sunshine and the lively colors of the painted buildings.

Fine bridges built across the Arno, magnificent road-ways, and
elegant houses, characterize the modern as well as the ancient
splendor of Pisa.

When we say "Deserted Pisa," we realize her sublime contrasts.
No more the enthusiastic crusader departs from her shores for the
fields of Asia: no more are brought in return the gold and ivory
and purple of the East: the saracens, who trembled on the coast of
Africa, fear not now her gleaming lances.

Where now the mystic painters and masters of *mosaic*, who enriched her monuments with the brilliant stones of Constantinople, and adorned her walls with the exquisite designs of their genius? Where now those men of finest perception—John of Pisa, and Nicholas—who chiseled her rare marbles, and polished them to splendor? They were to her as the "dawn ere the day," introducing her era of inspiration. She is now, principally, the refuge of the invalid who is soothed by her solitude, and protected by her mountains from the keen winds of the north. Pathetically sublime, she is indeed, "Deserted Pisa."

NOTE 11—PAGE 25.

Grand Campo Santo's Sculptured arches claim.

The Campo Santo is the most beautiful solemnity of Pisa, and appropriately located in its most lonely district.

It has been a cemetery for the last seven centuries.

It is a vast square enclosure, surrounded by high walls, with severe narrow entrances; but within, it is dazzlingly splendid with marbles, and paintings and sweet foliage—a dream of ecstasy to the antiquarian, a shrine for the study of the artist, a place of meditation forever. Its architect was "John of Pisa;" and the holy earth which first covered it for the reception of the *Dead*, was borne in ships from Jerusalem.

There are four Gothic galleries covered in rich abundance with luminous large frescoes. Some of the statuary and tombs present varied and thoughtful contrasts. Here are preserved the pathetic appeal, and response of the Renaissance: Endymion sleeps on the marbles of Campo Santo, while Diana kisses his forehead with as much devotion, as the cavalier of the thirteenth century who also kneels upon the marbles and prays not to the gods of pagan antiquity.

The head of Achilles, and the Bacchantes with their empty cups, and the Byzantine virgins, and the prophets, and the evangelists, are here in artistic and innocent confusion.

Here is the Holy Mother of Love; and here is Venus, the grace of Love:—when the gods took refuge, for the last time, in the Pantheon, they left some of their overlasting protests and appeals to the christian world, in the Campo Santo.

NOTE 12.—PAGE 26.

The gorgeous festivals of Lupercal,

Lupercal, an ancient Roman *festival*, was observed on the fifteenth day of February, in honor of the god Pan.

After the usual sacrifices, the bloody knife was touched to the foreheads of two illustrious youths who smiled at the moment of this performance; after which, the blood was wiped away with a

piece of soft wool dipped in milk. The skins of the animals sacri-
ficed were cut into thongs which were made into whips for the
youths who were then stripped almost naked; and, armed with
the whips, freely attacked all whom they met in the streets.

There were significant blessings and observances attached to re-
ceiving the lashes by special recipients, particularly, women. The
Greek name of Pan was *Lycœus,* from *Lukos,* a wolf; and its origin
may be, therefore, still more remote than the Roman one under
mention. Pan, who was god of the shepherds in Arcadia, protected
the sheep from the rapacity of the wolves.

Plutarch mentions these *festivals* as similar to those of the
Lycœan festivals in Arcadia; and that they were first adopted by
the Romans in honor of *Lukos,* a wolf, which cherished Romu-
lus and Remus. The priests who officiated in the Lupercalia were
called *Lupuci.* Pan was also one of the eight principal gods of the
Egyptians, worshiped under the form of a sacred goat; the death of
this animal was attended by universal mourning and a profound
fear; from which, the word *panic* is supposed to be derived.

Note 13.—Page 32.

Bound as to Sethon, to his life that wrong,

Sethon was the king of Egypt after the death of Anysis. He was
attacked, and strongly bound by the Assyrians; but his mysterious
power was wonderful, owing to the fact of his being a favorite priest
of Vulcan:—a number of rats came in the night, and knawed the
thongs which bound him. His powerful enemy found their arms
useless after one night, and their captive miraculously delivered.

In remembrance of this remarkable circumstance, a statue of
Sethon represented him with a rat in his hand, and bearing the inscription:—*Whoever fixes his eyes upon me, let him be pious.*

Note 14.—Page 38.

Unto the Sylva, then they took him:—Fate

The Sylva of the Dead, or the common cemetery, is, apart from
its customary awe, a startling and interesting spot of record in the
history of Palermo—it being the place fixed upon for the culmination of the Sicilian vespers. In those times, it was a place of
worship.

The Sylva is a large enclosed field, outside the town, regularly
planted with the somber and beautiful cypress, and containing an
elegant, little Gothic Chapel in the midst.

Before the cholera of 1837, it was used as the burial-place solely
of the poor; but, at this time, its undiscriminating and terrible
repose was varied by costly monuments of the rich. The particular features of its arrangements previously, were 366 slabs, in-
tended to be opened, one every day, and numbered for the days of

the year—therefore, each one was opened only once a year. Here were also some entrances to the chambers and galleries of the catacombs, the principal of which led from below the chapel as described.

NOTE 15.—PAGE 41.

The people of Messina fly to us—

In this revolution, Messina was, of all the towns of Sicily, one of the greatest sufferers—it was reduced to ruins. The scenes were terrible—burning hospitals with their inmates—panic stricken fugitives, vainly seeking refuge on board the English vessel, to be repulsed and sent back to the enemy. Two battalions of young men, aged only from sixteen to twenty, sustained the first effort against the enemy, "falling one after another without yielding an inch—only eight remained out of two thousand." In the affecting words of an eye witness: "I was moved to tears when they presented themselves to the ministry, bearing their banner, saying, 'Here is our banner ! we have been butchered ! but we have saved our honor !' "

NOTE 16.—PAGE 46.

Those men of Fate! O Palmerston! what use

The duplicity, and reactionary policy of Palmerston in those momentous days, were wrathfully deprecated by most of the Italian people: he made them many sanguine promises on behalf of their hoped for assistance from the English government, which he never fulfilled; thereby, leading them to postpone eventful efforts at propitious times, and otherwise misleading their expectations, and throwing them off their guard, while he secretly opposed the Parliament of Sicily that had declared King Ferdinand II and his dynasty to have forfeited the throne of Sicily forever. This secretive and double-dealing play of confiding resources, and interested opposing motives, cannot here be explained in detail. They were, however, sufficient for the time being to controvert the trusting patriots, and to render, subsequently, more deep and bitter the determined efforts of the revolution for the union of Italy.

NOTE 17.—PAGE 48.

Sbirri are knocking at the Sylva's gate:

Sbirri is the name of the Italian police. The chief of them, at the period mentioned, was Maniscalco in Sicily—and Satriano in Naples. Pontillo, Bruno, and others whose names were the terror of the country, were their brutal and remorseless assistants.

NOTE 18.—PAGE 48.

They'll knock down all the dead, until they meet

The intricacies of construction displayed in the catacombs of Rome, Naples and Palermo, have been minutely described by trav-

elers. The peculiarity, here mentioned, of the stone niche containing the standing body of the dead, being so adapted to turn
on a secret pivot, is not uncommon: the interminable galleries and
subterranean corridors, sometimes expanding into wide chambers
or chapels, are often thus intricately connected by unexpected
door-ways, places of ingress and egress not generally known, and
not often used since the days of the christian martyrs, except in
times of revolutionary disturbance, by the initiated—as hiding
places, etc.

NOTE 19.—PAGE 50.

Each one of whom in turn to other men

The organizations known as the Carbonari were divided, and
subdivided into comitatos of ten—each man being the head of
another ten. In this way, the indefatigable and enthusiastic mem-
bers were spread over all Italy, numbering thousands upon thousands, all secretly devoted to the one cause—a constitution of the
people and the regeneration of Italy—and owing a general amenity
to one head, or central comitato.

NOTE 20.—PAGE 51.

Halting, they found themselves upon a mount—

Monto Cuccio, a mountain four miles from Palermo. It is said
to have been a volcano, but this is not certain. On the top of
Monto Cuccio, are still seen the ruins of a fine castle, built by
William the First. Its beautiful frescos remain on the lonely and
dilapidated walls. It is probable, that in former times, its inmates
had knowlege of, and access to the neighboring and secret entrance
of the catacombs.

NOTE 21.—PAGE 58.

Of gloried, lonely, ancient Selinon;
And near the tomb-built chamber of Theron:—

Skirting the picturesque coast of Sicily from Palermo to the ruins of Selinon, are many pretty little towns, winding roads, and
ancient quarries. The ruins of Selinon are also called *Pileri*,
owing to its numerous pillars and monumental aspect—having the
appearance of a populous city when approached from a distance.
It is reached from Marsala, after passing through the smaller towns
of Mazara, Campo Bello, and Castel Vetrano. First, outside of
Marsala, comes the town of Luna, a stopping place for the muleteers from Marsala, generally laden with Barilla and grain for
Mazara. They do not ride, but walk beside their animals from the
towns of interval along their route. These muleteers are a cheer-
ful, adventurous set of fellows who are pleasant to fall in with,
beguiling the tedium of journey, with traditional stories and interludes of sweet, wild, mountain song.

San Giuliano is about half way from Marsala to Mazara: near
San Giuliano stands an old tower called Torre Silulina—nothing .

more is known of its name or history. Here is also cape Fero, the nearest rocky point to Africa. The white sails of the fishers' boats around the cape, can be seen when coming in from the fear of the clouds. At this place, the coast is low on the town of Mazara. The latter town is full of old ruins and relics of Saracenic interest. ; The Saracens landed here in 828, under Alcamæ who burned his boats after landing.

Outside the walls of Mazara, is Castel Vetano. The traveler may go in a *Feendaco* to the quarries in the neighborhood, from which the stones were taken for the ancient town of Selinon. Marshes in the vicinity of the sea render Campo Bello a sickly place. In those remarkable quarries, short pieces and architraves are still projecting from the banks of rock, as they were at first left unfinished by the workers, twenty hundred years ago. The compact, yellow stone of these quarries was called *Latoima*, by the Greeks. Campo Bello is the barony of the Duke of Leone, who lives in Naples. Eight miles more of rugged road, woody country, and splendid sunlight on the sea, and behold—the ruins of Selinon rising from the solitary waste, but, as before observed, appearing like a populous town when seen from a distance, and called by the natives "Pileri di Castel Vetrano." The town of Selinon was situated on two hills now interspersed with melancholy fragments of great size. The eastern hill commands a view of the place and the sea, with an abrupt incline towards the beach; and displaying, along the plane of its summit, the prostrate vestiges of three temples which lie in a parallel. line from north to south, distant forty feet from each other—simple, massive, austere Doric. Of those portions, fronting east, the one nearest the sea is 190 feet long and 72 feet broad, with beautiful, fluted columns; The center temple is less in size than either of the others. The northeast one is the largest. The celebrated one of Jupiter Olympús has eight columns in front and seventeen at the sides. This was mentioned by Diodorus, and Herodotus. It contained the statue of Bacchus with head, hands, and feet of ivory. Parts of two shafts, one in the portico and the other in the side, only remain standing, of this great temple. Hannibal's fires destroyed Selinon. A lonely watchtower stands by the sea, and a bridge, which were built of stones from the temples.

Cactus, Palmetto, and thistles interspersed by the mule-roads from the mines, cover this ancient district. Near by, is the river Canna, and the dilapidated castle of Chiarmonte, and the sea to the south, eight miles to the port of Girgenti, or ancient Akragas. Four miles to the town, from the port, by a hilly road lined with aloes and cactus and fruit trees. As the traveler leaves Selinon, the golden light of evening falls over the rich brown masses of ruins that crown the undulating eminences; and their splendid gloom follows his meditative thoughts.

Theron was one of the earliest governors of Sicily, and was paid divine honors after his death. His tomb is also one of the ancient relics of this templed and picturesque coast. It is twenty nine and a half feet in height, composed of two stones—the lower one is of pyramidal form, thirteen feet at the base, and nine, at the top; supporting a second, decorated with Ionic pillars at the corners, and a window in the center. Within, is a vault ground floor, or Ionic chamber; and a small stairs of communication with another chamber above.

When uninjured, with its inscriptions and ornaments, it was very beautiful, as also its situation classic and solemn—a grove of trees in front, and the temple of Concord in the distance.

NOTE 22.—PAGE 66.

White Pyramids by Sulphur mines.

In some of the mountainous districts of Sicily, Sulphur mines are numerous. their existence usually betokened by little mounds at their mouths.

Their appearance in the rays of the setting sun has a peculiar and beautiful effect. They can be seen at a great distance, from their sloping grassy expanse; and appear as though the golden beams of sol had been carelessly thrown on those summits, and lay there, glinting from millions of points, in reflective splendor.

NOTE 23.—PAGE 71.

And old Segesta's Temples bare,

There is only one magnificent temple of Segesta, or Ægesta, remaining. The other ruins consist of a theatre, broken pillars, capitols cornices, and rubbish, overgrown with weeds. The road leading to it from Palermo, from which it is distant some five or six miles, passes Morreale, Calatifini, and other small rural towns. Ægesta is mentioned by Diodorus, and Thucidides, who claim it to have Trojan origin. Its temple seems to have been stupendous in size, and possesses, at least, the prestige of thirty centuries—simple and grand, even after the lapse of ages. It stands on a slight elevation surrounded by its ruins and overgrown with weeds and grass, where goats that might be the very descendants of Pan, choose their dainty footsteps through intricate places—otherwise the lonely desolation of centuries impresses all around with the gloom and solemnity of death. Here, over broken pillars and fragments, a city once stood. The temple is two hundred feet in length, seventy in breadth, and sixty in height. It is now roofless, and is in form, a parallelogram. The material of which it was built was a sort of calcareous stone, though now so blackened and dimmed by time. It was once, probably, freshly bright from the numerous yellow quarries that abound in that district.

Thirty-six columns, each six feet in diameter, supporting an ornamental frieze, stood on four large steps. On another elevation, or little hill, called Varvarro, stood the theatre, of which, the foundation only, of the outer wall remains. Its area is also filled with the relics of its fallen splendor now overgrown with wild Thyme that presses out, beneath the footsteps, its pathetic sweetness on the desolate air.

NOTE 24.—PAGE 77.

From Olevano—the great mounts, between:

As a mere mountain, Vesuvius, the greatest of these, is not perhaps remarkable except for the awful associations of the ages which belong to it. The great and terrible *genius* of death, so long silent, with recollective regret, as it were, for his former destruction, over the desolation of Pompeii and Herculaneum!

Vesuvius is 3800 feet high; and the fears entertained of its future destructiveness give it a vivid and awful interest.

How dreadful to conjecture that Naples may one day, share the fate of those cities of the past: may not the monster, so warily slumbering now, be at the same time nursing his secret fires for a more signal exhibition of demoniac wrath than he has yet displayed?

NOTE 25.—PAGE 77.

Cozenza; in God's name, and by our love,

The devoted and heroic wives and families of the Italian patriots have been, not the least, sufferers in the successive revolutions that have consigned to the page of history, as traitors or martyrs, the illustrious names of the contending inaugurators. From the days of Fiesco and Doria in Genoa, to those of more recent strife, this pathetic and secondary woe is inseparable from the radiance and the glory of achievement, and alike, from the despair of disaster.

NOTE 26.—PAGE 92.

Indomitable way;—in ev'ry room,

The city of Palermo had been bombarded several days: the banks containing the valuables of the poor had been burned; and some of the most peaceful and religious of the people, were butchered in their own convents. The street scenes were terrible! Sometimes a priest might be seen, raised on the shoulders of the people, cursing the king, exonerating, justifying, and blessing the people, and advocating their continued efforts until a constitution would be accorded them, despite the lying subterfuges and delays of the arch traitor, "king Bomba." Occasionally, a forty-eight pounder would be discovered among the rocks near an old fort, or buried somewhere. This, mounted upon an ox-cart, was dragged by the hands

of the desperate and enthusiastic people into the city. One such
was placed during the night on the bastion of Porta Montaldo, an
old bulwark of the city, which could enfilade the bastion of the
Palazzo Reale.

The 25th of January 1848 was a day of memorable conflict: the
Palazzo Reale was a large and handsome edifice—a combination of
Saracenic, and Norman style. Its site was, formerly, the residence
of the Carthagenian, Roman, and Saracen governors. It lay on
the western extremity of the walled city, between the two gates,
Porta Nuova and Porta Montaldo. On the side, fronting the city,
there were at that time, flanking the three gates, two large forts,
armed with thirty six heavy cannons. In the rear were a rampart
and a moat. The large square in front contained the fortified
places; *S. Elis Abbetta,* southward; *Speala le Civico,* eastward; and
S. Giacomo, northward. The people attacked these formidable
positions with ingenuity and sublime courage. As these buildings
were in continuation with others, holes were made from house to
house through the walls, every room being the scene of bloody
strife, while the soldiers contended hand to hand.

Note 27.—Page 95.

The next time that Morbili came, he brought,

The duke Morbili was the ubiquitous Satellite of Del Caretto
and the king. He was also the terror of Naples, having risen to
favor through his assiduous and vile services:—a fire or any other
calamity in those days of his malicious exertions, was not a less
welcome visitant to any one subject to his covert supervision.

Note 28.—Page 102.

His minious sought her in the *barathrum.*

The horrors of the ancient Roman prisons are indescribable.
There was in some of them a sort of trap-door, or hole in the floor
of an inner prison made after the plan of the Tullianum and the
ancient prisons of Smyrna. In the acts of Pionius, and others,
these are described, where the jailors "shut them up in the inner
part of the prison, so that bereaved of all comfort and light, they
were forced to sustain extreme torment from the darkness and
stench. These pits or trapdoors were often nothing less than
openings to cess-pools, or the common sewer, and prisoners were
sometimes dispatched by being cast headlong into them.—

Note 29.—Page 115.

Feronia Goddess bright: thy sacred woods

Feronia, was principally the Goddess of manumitted slaves, who
obtained their liberty by being seated in her chair,—on which

these words were inscribed—"Bene meriti servi sedeant; surgant liberi." Her Temple was near Mount Soracte in Latium, where there was a town called by her name; saered woods were her particular delight, and fountains in which her votaries washed their hands and faces at solemn festivals. Those inspired with the spirit of this Goddess, could walk barefoot over burning coals without injury.

NOTE 30.—PAGE 116.

Fides! the oaths of honesty were kept.

Fides was the Goddess before whom the Romans registered their oaths and made vows of Fidelity. Numa was the first who ordered divine honors to be paid.

I am indebted for many of the details and descriptions in the preceding notes to Castelar's "Old Rome and New Italy," W. F. Cummings', "Notes of a Wandérer," and to an old "History of Sicily" London edition,—by an English Army officer, its modest Author's name or identity not otherwise given.

Nonnenwerth,

A LEGEND OF THE RHINE.

REVISED AND ILLUSTRATED.

SECOND EDITION.

ADVERTISEMENT.

"Nonnenwerth, a Legend of the Rhine," is founded upon one of the most beautiful and romantic traditions. The scenes are laid in the latter part of the eighth century. The unhappy Hildegarde was the Lady of Heligoland, and was betrothed to Roland the Nephew of Charlemagne. Roland was ordered to the wars by his uncle the king: this was on the eve of their marriage which was postponed until his return.

In vain she waited, and he came not: an occasional pilgrim's return brought her only indefinite tidings.

The duplicity of Lupo and Hunald may, or may not, be true: I have introduced it, to give some vivid realism to the cause of Hildegarde's sad resolution. Lupo and Hunald are, however, the real names of two remorseless enemies of Roland—no doubt, the principal of those at whose hands he afterwards met his death at Roncesvalles.

The "Arch of Rolandseck" only remains of the once strong and magnificent castle built by Roland. He chose for its site the pinnacle of Roderberg overlooking the Rhine. From its watch-towers could also be seen the lake, and the convent of Nonnenwerth in which his promised bride, believing him to be dead, immured herself previous to his long delayed return from the crusades.

Roland was the son of Milo, Count of Angiers, and Bertha, sister of Charlemagne. The word "Paladin," or "Palatine," afterward so common in poetry as a characteristic designation of the warriors of Charlemagne, was first applied to Roland and his followers, by a Saxon poet who wrote in the reign of the Emperor Arnulphus, about seventy years after the death of Charles. In the dells of the Pyrenees, is yet shown a flower called the Casque de Roland; and a steep and rugged defile in the Crest of the mountain is pointed out as the "Breche de Roland." Here, also, in the last century, stood a small chapel, in the immediate neighborhood of Roncesvalles, which tradition affirms to be the resting place, of the chiefs, who, together with Roland, comprising in all thirty knights of the Palace, fell victims to that memorable and treacherous the attack of the Gascons. Thirty tombs without inscriptions were to be seen in the vicinity; and a quantity of bones was shown in a cave under the chapel. I have retained the precise identity of this spot, though three others in the locality are pointed out and severally claimed as the burial place of Roland. What earth is specially incorporated with the clay of the hero matters not, and is probably unknown.

"Thy crumbling Arch yet stands, O Rolandseck;
 Far up the rocky steep, of Drachenfels;
 There thrills the music of the streams that break
 Their broad paths down to where the blue Rhine swells."

Page 137.—Stanza I.

NONNENWERTH.

A LEGEND OF THE RHINE.

I.

WHY crumbling arch yet stands, O Rolandseck!
  Far up the rocky steep of Drachenfels;
There thrills the music of the streams that break
Their broad paths down to where the blue Rhine
  swells.
Cold are the craters of thy centuries!
Where Palatines have marched, thy paths are peace;
And thy green willows are yet dense in dells,
Whence Charlemagne's gold banners and bright
  shields
Went forth to glorious strife on Syrian fields.

II.

Fire-born the lava of thy seven heights!
Along the river castled turrets rise;
There clings the ivy on the tinted blights,
Soundless and luminous in evening skies:
Repose hath starlight and the mingling wave,
Decay hath sunlight and the voiceless grave!

While no clashed cimeter to shield replies,
No charger's footsteps near thy fountains fall,
No revel holdeth in thy roofless hall !
Lonely and voiceless now, from time's recall.

III.

How shall we bring the records back, of days
Glad with the laugh, and love, and eyes of life ?
The joyous brows that won their knightly bays ?
The free high worth of peace, the strength of strife ?
The swan-like throats of music that have sung ?
The deep vein'd, fine soft glances that have flung
Sweet souls into each other, and made rife
Their story with thine ages, freighted years,
So long since gone with tributes and with tears ?

IV.

Thy trees have fallen down to silent caves,
Thy floors of stone shut in the graves of men;
Rude piles make echoes from the troubled waves
When winter night and storm return again :
These are of things not lost where Roland was—
Roland of crest, and lance, and bannered cross !
One of the kingly men who said to pain,
Thy tomb's a beauteous toy, and lo ! the stone,
That rolls away from thee, is called a crown !

V.

The crystal key of contemplation turns
In the fine lock of auspices, create
With the old dust of time's uncovered urns,
Blown sea-ward unto thee, O Golden Gate ! [1]

Not of thee, Shasta! high, unsullied peak!—
No records hath it, of thy light pure snow,—
No armor-laden men, grown faint and weak—
There gladly lying down while life ebbed low!
Thy grand Columbian barriers ne'er fell
Before invading footstep; and there lies
No shield or corselet buried in the swell
Of thy proud, stainless waters where they rise,
That like a quick steed who abjures the spur,
Boundeth the rocks among on freedom's way,
Below the bending pine and swaying fir,
And the white feathery foam and dashing spray,
Down to the fields of wheat and valley grass,
Down to the widening shore past flowering meads—
No fierce Thermopylæ soiled any pass   .
With vain, dead-hates of conquests or of greeds.

VI.

So we are glad! but as with deepening tone
Of low sweet music, and of garlands flung
Before some pale, sad cortege that alone
Treads a dark pathway, so have mourners sung!

VII.

The Camp of Charlemagne.

The night had come! Mons Jovis under snow![2]
And the high calm's illimitable glow
Of all the midnight heaven looked, as when
Hannibal rested with his weary men
Around the Temple whose dark walls then leaned

Against the great acclivity, half screened
From the loud winds of Clusa—while in sleep
All the still camp whose onward march would
    sweep
O'er Lombard cities, a dread destiny,—
Verona's—Pavia's sieges yet to be.

VIII.

The king watched late while others slept: he
    thought
Of the high plans his future actions wrought;
And at the morn, Duke Bernard's armor came
Across the mount which keeps his lasting name:
A grand reunion in the valley made
Each equal glorious march, a toil repaid,
With Charles, the greatest monarch of the Franks:
Villages, castles, towns, along the banks
Of Alps and river, on the path he went,
Rose not with moan of grief, or heart's lament,—
Not as to despot on his rampart way;
But with most welcome gladness, gathered they,
Bringing the palm branch, and the rose, and bay:
Nor were they sullen at Mons Cinisus;
With anthems, him they met, and raised the Holy
    Cross.

IX.

And here, with greeting, ere he pitched his tent,
Where the great mountains in the valley blent—
An Envoy of the East, most stately, sent—
In gold and silver garments, rich arrayed—

Loaded with presents, while eight cymbals played
The hour, in which the King his audience made:
With brazen bells and heralds, the advance
Proclaimed a host, with pennon and with lance,
And gleamed their burnished spears, like moving
    flame,
As slowly nearer to the camp, they came:—
And standing, Haroun's envoy thus addressed
The mighty Emperor of all the West:—
" My voice, O King, this hour, is Haroun's will—
Not as to Christian, Hebrew, Moslem—still,
To thy own greatness only, would he turn
As the Nile's lotus where the sun doth burn :
And to the worth of all thy famous deed,
Which many glorious ends may still fulfill,
This adulation is his gracious meed
That I bear unto thee, and here concede."

X.

This said, his servant drawing near unrolled
Fine silks, and talmas made of cloth of gold—
Byzantine fabrics from the cities old:[3]
Pure balms, and ointments, and most sweet
    perfumes,
Made from the rarest flowers of Eastern blooms;
A curious bronze clock—twelve bright balls fell,
In just the number that, the hour, might tell;
On a gold cymbal they were caught below,
As many as the dial marked did show;
Its figures, windows, through which horsemen rode
From some inside mysterious abode
Of clockwork deftly made—it is presumed

They were crusaders mailed and richly plumed—
But what their separate titles, ranks, or names,
Since time remote, no deep conjecture frames;
But, by all this, we know that model clocks,
In *this* more modern day of mines and stocks,
Tell not more nicely, morning, night, or noon,
Than Charlemagne's clock did—gift from Haroun:
So strangely wrought and finely gilt, the whole—
That, of some magic life, it seemed the soul.

XI.

And last presented in her august grace—
The guards wide parted to make clear her place—
A large white elephant, as wholly white
As late-bathed plumes of swans at early flight :
Ah ! we can tell not of her perfect praise,
Taught, of the sun's warm travel, all the ways:
Endearing things they said along the line,
She seemed to hear; and shed, like beams of wine,
A wordless answer in her eyes and mien,—
A sacred symbol there among them seen,
An Indian goddess of *Tanjore's* great shrine:
And she had for a present, a large tent,
On her soft shoulders, folded as she went—
Remarkably constructed, its light form,
But most impervious to the sun or storm;
And, bearing it, she knelt before the King:
—The canopy was costly she did bring,
In colors fine embroidered, flower and bird—
And startled antelopes, a fleeing herd—
And from the Koran, many a sacred word,

Mid radiating rays of Persia's sun—
And from the mountains, how the Ganges run—
And Himalayan peaks of towering height,
Whose scintillating crowns of fadeless white
Seemed to touch skies of lambent sapphire light;
And starry-studded, rubies mingled there—
And *Houris* listening to the moslem's prayer,
The kneeling suppliant's lifted eyes on high—
"A thing of beauty" was this canopy:
The mosque's gold dome, from which *Muezzins* call
At sunset, devotees—displaying all:—
"*Bismillah!* Come ye forth! Harken, the chime!
Mahomet is God's prophet for all time!"
The splendid spire and crescent's silver gleam,
Worked in its fabric, as in sleep a dream:
"This for thy war tent on the mount and plain,
O King of all the Lombards, Charlemagne!
And may'st thou live forever to enjoy!"
—Thus ended the fair speech of the envoy,
As set, behind the mount, the sun's last beam.

XII.

The listening King was pleased.   With quiet joy
He answered: "Tell your monarch of the East
That his fair message shall my thoughts employ:
In turn, I wish the christians there released—
I will send back with thee a Frankish priest,
And many Counts of retinue and state,
Who will more definitely *this* relate;
And still assure him that as for the rest—
Reciprocal regard, I do attest:

He is as I,—he hath most rapid zeal,
And energy as bold as that I feel—
Magnificent designs, and mind as free,
For these, most high esteem he holds with me;
I greet thee in his name, high embassy !
In my wide, jovial camp, take needful rest,
As may seem fitting to a royal guest—
With recreation and all soft repose
That easy pastimes and thy will propose."
At this he bowed and turned: as he arose,
A Syrian monk that waited, now came near—
His firm demeanor modest and not bold,
But with such mild obeisance as of old:—

XIII.

"Sire, in thy favor wilt thou justly hear?
I seek thy gracious audience without fear—
Thou listest all thy people may disclose :
They send thee greeting, where blooms Sharon's
    rose,
And ask through me thy intermediate aid—
Now at thy feet, is supplication laid:
The journey's plaint I make, is sadly told,
Since seventy thousand dinars, tax in gold,
Each year at Bagdad—for a bonded sun
In Syria shines, the tomb of Christ, upon.
Oh ! in the splendor of thy royal name,
State unto Haroun that 'tis cause of blame;
And for thy friendly care he will requite
Unto thy Christian sons, this tribute's right."

XIV.

With courteous words the monarch acquiesced;
And, glancing o'er his knights in earnest quest,
Singled out Roland from the pageant throng—
Among the beautiful most fair and strong:
Had he such heavy brows as though the stroke
Of Jove's long-fallen bolt, there striking, broke;
While in the beauty of his grave lips' peace,
Love turned itself as doth sweet sound in seas:
Forward he came with radiance just subdued—
His was the fervor of that quiet mood—
As of the Spartans, it is said, no sounds
Of drum or trumpet filled their battle grounds:
They needed not, to rouse their valor's will,
Aught but the touch of lyre, or lute's sweet thrill;
Because, within them, their own souls did fill
Strong harmonies, from deep confineless bounds:
With rested lance he bowed touching the mane
Of his fine charger, and arose again,
With ready hand upon the golden rein.

XV.

Then seemed the King to give command alone,
But much of tender pride its undertone—
For this fair nephew was the favored one:
"Canst thou, O Roland, find Anselmo, and
With ninety Counts depart for Holy land?
Tell the good priest that I such message send
As you have heard ere now, unto the end—
This to the mighty Caliph: that he move
His heart of mercy, for my heart of love:
  *10

And give my Christian people, long denied,
The freedom of the gates where Jesus died."

XVI.

Three Squires gathered at a herald's call,
Amarin, Sarron, and brave Andiol—
These were the leaders of Count Roland's men
By mountain fastness and Pyrenean glen—
To whom he gave his uncle's orders:—then
The day of journey with import arrayed—
So long anticipated, often stayed—
With still some unforeseen event, delayed:
Each cavalier's proud grace, each lance in rest,
Plumed helmet, visor closed, cuirass on breast,
And silken scarfs fair fingers had caressed
While twining o'er the shoulder or the arm,
With tears and smiles of love, bedewed to charm
The pain of parting —the dread change of chances,
Could these soft things protect from Paynim
    lances
The hearts beneath them, beating fond and true?
The daring hearts of Mowbray, Walter, Hugh,
Daubeny, Ralph, and Philip — all Knights
    Templar—
Each one the flower of chivalry—exemplar
Of deeds heroic on fame's after page!
—Its centuries a decade from their Age.

XVII.

Peace to their ashes, under Syrian palms!
There still the Arab rests to make *salaams*,
And cites the story-tellers, gone before,

With coffee cups and *chibouks* o'er and o'er,
The great disastrous flight, Noureddin had—
And here the story-tellers turn more sad—
But telling always their traditions, right;
Alternate victory, defeat, and flight:
And so they tell, most sadly, truly, this
While sleep the camels near the oasis,
With faces westward to the very place he
Had come from—Templar Knight, Gilbert DeLacy,
Who, while the darkness into blackness blent,
Surprised Noureddin in his mighty tent.[5]
—That night, Mahomet fiery angels sent
To bear Noureddin up to Paradise
Where *Houris* wept o'er him with tender eyes:
—While swift the victor linking, like a wreath,
The broken cimeter upon the sheathe
Of his great Frankish sword—he bore it far—
Its jeweled hilt, bright gleaming, like a star,
A bloody trophy of the moslem war.

XVIII.

The Parting of Roland and Hildegarde.

But I have mused too long, o'er foreign lands,
And told to soon, the story of their years—
Forgetting the brave knights' conjoining bands,
And their fair "Lady-loves" in smiles and tears!
—But while they gathered all, one rode apart,
Not least in valor, but most sad at heart:
We shall know what he did—that eve he went

To make a sweet farewell, when skies were blent
With the late day's deep purple and red gold,
And from the fields the lambs hied to their fold;
Almost inaudible his stepping steed
That bruised the dewy perfumes on the mead :
—Into the mountains rode he shortly then,
Where the dark cypress waved in every glen—
Each dun, dread precipice in sombre calm
Held the grapes ripening, while ethereal balm,
With gifts of fire, as hearts with visions blending,
Fed them from rocks, on which they grew de-
    pending
Like webs in winter, rock to rock enlaced; [6]
O'er the basaltic walls, the vine stems traced,
Where green their garlands in the summer hung:
Along the eddying stream their leaves were flung—
Great terraces of gloom, or vernal sheen,
Above the winding river grandly seen.

XIX.

A bridge across the Nahe near Bingen stands;
Beneath it, soft waves over shining sands,
With many arches pillared, grand and old—
Onward from thence, the road to Niederwald:
Here Roland lingering rode and hastened not,
His pace in keeping with his saddened thought,
In fancy listening to each fairy grot
Below the little stones whose murmurs made
Indefinite, strange sounds that chainless strayed:—
These were the haunting Gnomes of Whisperthal, [7]
Dwelling in small cascades of pebbly fall—

"A bridge across the Nahe near Bingen stands;
Beneath it, soft waves over shining sands,
With many arches pillared, grand and old—
Onward, from thence, the road to Niederwald:"

Page 148.—Stanza XLV.

Their voices wierdly unto him did call:
" Return, delay! O Roland, do not pass!
The Lorch lies in the sun, Roland, alas!
All the dreamy day in cymar of gold,
The Lurly maiden sits where cliffs are cold;
Swiftly her white hands in the sunset shine,
With gleaming golden comb and tresses fine:
Thou knowest well the lifted eyes that haunt
Her wondrous, manifold, sweet, thrilling chant—
Roland! return, delay! Oh, do not pass!
The sounding falls are near, Roland, alas!"

XX.

But soon to silvery beechwoods he had come,
Where summery bee and flower with wings and
    hum,
Changed the dark current of his thought's day-
    dream;
A fading, dim perception it did seem
To an o'er anxious passion of forethought,
With hope, and fear and tenderness enwrought.
"Ah! such," he mused, "is the proud soul's dis-
    guise—
Who will admit fate takes him by surprise?
And we are pleased with such imaginings—
To hold its wayward reins, to plume its wings—
Or, out of long sweet sighs, to charm a strain
For festal, deep repeatings of such pain,
Some way to wear the soul, than it is worn—
Yet always seen, the forehead and the thorn!
Oh, I shall see her weep for this, I fear!

Thou, rose of fragrance, needest not a tear,
Since dew-falls, nightly to thy full heart come:
My fathers! dare I wish these lips were dumb,
That oft with clarion deeds thy names, recalled?
How shrink they now at this sweet love, appalled!"

XXI.

Gone are thine ivied years, sad, lone and fleet—
And of their things, long lost, the bowered seat
Near a grey lintel, where sat Hildegarde:.
The lintel there is yet time-stained and marred;
And all the lofty Keep of Ehrenfels,
Whose roofless walls amid the forest stand— 8
Their tumbled fragments dimly, darkly grand:
Near by, the beautiful and blue Moselle's
Bright, limped waves are flowing to the Rhine,
As though no note were kept of ruin's sign:
A peasant guide walks there to-day, and tells
How many hundred years have made it old,
In those dense oaken glooms of Niederwald:
—Strangers oft rest beneath its beechen shade,
To view the beauties found in every glade;
And to the chapel on the hill-side climb,
Among the vineyards of sweet Rudesheim.

XXII.

That freighted hour he feared; his footstep stayed
Short of the moonlight on the open glade:
How should he comfort, in the sad ordeal,
The sorrow, half whose weight he too, must feel?
Ah, but the interludes of thought's excess—

These had not time to make it more nor less—
Some fervor, held just close to consciousness,
Made Hildegarde perceive that he was near—
His step—leaned forward, pausing—she might
  hear!
And straight she waited, listened, saw him clear:
Then hastening, but—why state with any word,—
To those who've mourned it, 'tis but anguish stirred,
Or as a touch rude on a sweet lute-chord—
To those who have not known it, 'tis but fraught
In words, with meanings pale, like statues wrought.

XXIII.

Let us not linger o'er what soon she knew:
At first, she scarce believed it could be true—
That they must part, that he should journey far,
O'er pathways distant unto dangerous war,
Or as the knightly envoy of the king—
But oh, what tidings might the future bring!
Anticipating all—dim, tear-wet lids,
Whose pride's supremacy, the tear forbids:
Then sudden quivering agony, all white—
Forgetting pride's commanding sense of right—
Quick pain, yea, quick, or it had killed her quite!
—What said he then? no word, but his light hand
Rested on hers, as silent he did stand.
" Oh, I had thought, with lute and garlands, thou
Would'st come, beloved, not, alas, as now!"
So near his restful shoulder—timid—yet,
Only her white hand on it lightly set,
She questioned not of love's repeated vow:

With resignation's smile and grief's release,
She now had come from struggle, into peace;
And touching her soft lips to his fair brow—
He kissed her with some quick, impulsive will—
And then, she leaned her head down and was still.

XXIV.

Oh, shadowy vail's foreboding, not revealed!
It breathed in his soft accents, and was sealed
In the firm, tearless glance of her dark eye,
The imposing calm's restraints of agony,
As those great, slumbrous banks of Indian palm,—
Along the low coast of Coromandel,
The spray, their nurture, and the Ocean's swell—
Are quiet near the coming of the sea,
Their deep roots in a reef's captivity,
While all the Monsoon's desert-laden balm
And burning winds sweep o'er them utterly.

XXV.

" My dear, when I am gone, beware Hunald!
Along the Spanish march, his deeds are told—
Reckless and subtile; violent and bold!
And of his kinsman Lupo, too, beware!
He gave me once a troth not free or fair—
Let them not injure thee, my flowret rare!"
" Yea, sweet," she said, " resigning thee, I will,
In all high faith's collectedness, fulfill
Thy love's behest, each day and hour I live,
While slow the long months pass, or long years
    grieve!
Yea, sweet, I am content through burning ill;

My soul hath its completeness : love will fill
Immortal aisles of heaven, though this earth,
With sounding waves of sea and clouds of dearth,
Whelm all its quivering throbs; and never pour,
Upon its censor fires, one token more."

XXVI.

Thrilled with remembrance of his sweet caress,
Then in her eyes of gentle smilingness,
Some high resolve whose deep flush filled her heart,
As when the sunset on the sea grows less
To splendors gathered, ere it all depart :
Buoyant and transient, were this charming force,
But for dominion of the mind's resource—
Its firmness and its tenderness one course,
Whose pause of love, these governed aspects bless,
Despite the heart's importunate distress
Of sweet contending powers, with wielding will
And some faint echo of the voice :—" Be still !"
Eternal starlight in the trembling air,
Thou art alone forever, everywhere !
—His foot departed from the marble stair,
This loneliness was hers—left standing there.

XXVII

But who were Hunald and the feared Lupo, [9]
In Roland's anxious thoughts, forecasting woe ?
They were the aids of treacherous deeds oft done,—
The wicked brother, and perfidious son
Of Abu Taurus, Saracen Emir—
Oft his Damascus blade's swift, fatal whirr,

Struck vainly, Roland's mirror-polished shield
In many a mountain breach, and valley field—
At last, twas Abu Taurus had to yield:
Then Pampeluna's jeweled medal bright,
Was struck for Roland's memorable fight:
The hostages, exacted, were these two;
Hunald and Lupo nearest—son and brother—
Than whom Taurus had given any other—
With tribute promised and submission true.

XXVIII.

In secret *not* submissive: every line
Of his dominions, he had to resign,
Contested hard, each Pyrenean province—
Their mutual valor well remembered since:
Yet, terms complied with, and rich tributes sent
By Abu Taurus to the kingly tent;
While many garrisons, had Charlemagne,
To keep submissive to his anxious reign,
The restless Emirs in subjection's chain—
From Biscay's bay, to Lyons' gulf, the whole
Of empire conquered had such armed control:
But still rebellious Lupo, and Hunald,
By Abu Taurus, to revolt, were called—
Till at most bitter cost, *all* Aquitaine
Was finally reduced by Charlemagne.

XXIX.

The Crusader's Journey.

The soft unfolding purple of the dawn—
Beyond the misty hills, like some vast throne—
Beyond the utmost mounts whose hamlets kept

The previous night late vigils and now slept :
At day, the files of burnished steel, aflame—
All musical with movement and the name
Of fair Jerusalem, advancing slow,
Like strong tides in deep unison, to flow
In one long segregated mass, the line—
Their standards eastwards turned to Palestine:
What ardor or what sorrow there was pent,
The martial trumpets drowned, enhanced, or lent
A last note of farewell—none should repine—
Bright waving hands, last looks—on march they
    went,
Kings, pages—all the knightly tournament.

XXX.

How, in high reverence were there unfurled,
Bright banners, faceward to the Eastern world:
Behind them, silence and their parting tears;
Before them, effort and, perhaps, long years ;
The green shore's murm'ring current, and the close
Of each long weary day to eve's repose ;
The ridge of rock, the story vale, the plain,
Some Gothic citadel—the vale again:
The straggling line of horse, the strongest few
Contending swift ahead for the first view:
—For every morn brought warmer skies more
    blue—
And holy scenes, historic childhood knew ;
And, every eve, some blessed spring or well,
Beside whose grassy rim they camped to tell
How many leagues were passed, how many yet

To Christian spire or Moslem minaret,
That, in the distance to their longing eyes,
Seemed with new hope replete or with surprise—
Each step so fondly marked in Holy Writ:
—After long hours of ride—resting at last,
Dismounted from their horses, they might sit
In shady dells the Maccabees had passed,[10]
Or view a castle old, 'twas said, they built—
Beside whose shrine they knelt, and kissed the
    Cross sword-hilt.

XXXI.

Mounted again—again the stony vale:
They journeyed mostly then at twilight pale :
Still intervening hills—there seemed no end:
The rocky landscape, up and down did blend:
Hills seemed to multiply beneath their feet—
The horses sometimes weary, sometimes fleet:
At last, an ancient castle's towers they saw—
They stopped a moment in subduing awe—
Reined in their bridles—gazing the first time
Upon Jerusalem, sacred—sublime !
—Not easy to describe the emotions' throng
Filling the Christian breast when, after long
And toilsome journeying, the olive shade
Gives welcome on the slopes of Gihon's glade—
The pools of Gihon where a King was crowned,[11]
The Bard of Canticles—each storied mound
Commands the battlements that rise above
The long desired—the city of their love :
" Jerusalem ! Jerusalem !" they said—

Not saying more : in transport's awe, dismayed,
Some wept in rapture on each other's breast;
And some, the sacred earth, low kneeling pressed.

XXXII.

They entered by the Bethlehem gate at noon,
When parleying with the guards had ended : soon
They found sweet rest by fount and Olive shade,
After the toil and dust of journey made,
Within the Latin Convent—guests they came,
With letters heralding their august fame;
But nought they saw, after that first, far view,
Could with such awe's impress, their souls imbue :
—Beside the roadway, on bright carpets spread,
Were groups of grave Turks sitting, each dusk head,
Bound with a turban rich of Persian stripes—
In silence, dignified, they smoked their pipes;
And old, white-bearded Jews, beneath the walls—
The glory of whose race, nought now recalls—
Dilating to diciples, of its splendor;
And with imposing glance, raised sadly tender,
In deprecation to the terraced tower,
O'er which the crimson flag of Turkish power,
Above the conquered city, heavy floating—
The Christians, not less sad, the emblem noting.

XXXIII.

Descending, from the convent, a steep hill,
At early morn they passed the holy door—
Its Gothic front and steps. the same, are still,
Where the long tides of constant ages pour :

About the courtway of the front and side—
A throng of various people, occupied:
There were some pious merchants selling beads[12]
And crucifixes, and such holy ware;
Some beggars in the court explained their needs:
Some early votaries were kneeling there:
The Turkish door-keepers had not arrived—
They kept the Church-keys as they're kept to-day—
So Roland and his comrades then contrived
To make the hours of waiting pass away,
With much comment on such restriction made:
Their presents on the Sepulchre were laid,
Together, with some alms, meant for the poor,
By passing them through holes made in the door—
This did the pilgrims too, who hither strayed:
The monks inside, received them, with a word
Of prayer or blessing, softly outside heard:
At last, the door was opened—helmets off,
And shoes; and turbans, did the pilgrims doff:
Mahomedan and Christian, Jew as well—
An equal reverence, each act did tell.

XXXIV.

Those trains of worshipers are passed away—
There, other trains of worshipers, to-day:
Pilgrim and priest, the holy slab, they kiss,
Is under hanging lamps, and polished is
With fine and sacred keeping; waxen light
Of three large tapers many feet in hight,
In front, and at the ends,—the lustrous gleam

Of that which lies below reflects each beam:
On *this*, was washed for burial, they explain,
The glorious body of the Lord, when slain.

XXXV.

The place in which the pious Empress sought
The Holy Cross long hidden from all view; [13]
When, with the crosses of the theives, 'twas
   brought—
Her anxious doubts, to know which one was true:
Pious Helena! thou art not alone!
The superscription broken off, and thrown
Into the town-ditch or a vault near by,
Too long forgotten, oft may careless lie:
But two were thieves' crosses—what verity?
Only a miracle could testify,
The one cross holiest, the sacred one
Whose beam owned the inscription; thou did'st try:
And for thy sake, this miracle was done:
—A noble lady sick and ill at at ease,
And long in suffering without hope or peace,
Thou did'st make touch it; and she was restored!
—A young man dead, and by his friends deplored,
Was ready, made for burial; but taken
Out and laid on it—lo, he did waken!
Forgive, all ye who may not this believe,
That I repeat it—I would not deceive!
Almost incredulous, perhaps, but still—
Still must the heart contend with reason's will,
These metaphysic miracles of truth,
I learned to love in faith's sweet days of youth!

XXXVI.

To other holy places Roland went,
At every shrine his knightly knee was bent;
In dismal chapels; over ancient tombs:
Where Arimathea's Joseph sleeps: the rooms
Built over these, so ancient holy spots,
Have not changed ought beneath them; the same
    grots
Hollowed in Calvary's unmelting rock:
The fissure still shown— of the earthquake shock—
That Roland's eyes looked on, as so ours might,
The subterranean chapel's gloomy light
Not all concealing it—as when Christ died—
From floor to ceiling up the chapel's side:
The stone on which the angel sat, when risen
The dead Lord, he had watched, three mournful
    days:
The hall of flagellation, and the prison
Of Peter; and the hollow, rocky place
Where they laid Jesus—*this* is rarely seen—
A marble altar, built o'er it, a screen.

XXXVII.

Before all these his meditations blent
With prayer and silence, until called—his tent
Was strapped for travel—to the Caliph's Court:
When at the Convent gate, blew loud and short,
A herald's bugle note. "Behold!" he said,
"'Tis Haroun comes himself through Gihon's glade,
With royal courtesy to wait on me:
My Squires! our journey's toil will needless be!

Let us go forth to meet him, where he comes,
With our own noble banners and brave plumes!
Not less must be our condescending state,
Nor less our consciousness of it!" Elate
And glad, the watchers viewing from the towers,
The royal traveler distant yet some hours,
They saw; then hastening, a selected band
Went forth to meet him—Roland in command.

XXXVIII.

And lo! what silver sheen neath azure skies
Glitters resplendent before Roland's eyes?
Can he believe his sight? An infidel
Raising the Christian standard to the swell
Of the upfloating, balmy, summer air?
He sees aright; in awful truth, 'tis there—
Its silken model hung with garlands rare:
The *Dead Christ* on the cross, in wreath of thorns—
This sign, 'tis known, the Mussulman ne'er scorns:
The *Heart of Mary, Mother*—seven swords,
Transfixed—all there portrayed:—some latin
     words: [14]
Two silver, pendant chains together meet,
Where hang three golden keys—O signs complete!
Ye mean the ransom of your sacred gates—
Your bloodless glory, upon Roland waits!

XXXIX.

"Behold! O Frankish chieftain! we are come
To give thee welcome, from thy western home!
Here are the Keys of Olivet's high dome,

11

Where solemn centuries have long reposed;
And to thy hand, is given, to be *closed*
Or *opened*, at thy will, the *Sacred Tomb!*"
Roland, at this, bowed low his sable plume—
Adoring awe shared on his face, sad gloom:
Haroun al Raschid knew, ere all expressed,
The pledged, devoted care that filled the breast
Of the fair, brave crusader—his request
Was thus complied with, graciously and soon:
They pitched their tents then, at the hour of noon,
And lingering, joyous, did the camps rejoice
By marble-margined founts with cascade voice,
And shaded plats of Olive—memories
Of sanctity and hospitable peace:
—Yea, though a stranger, so his task was told;
And Roland, faceward, turning to the west—
All haply ended his so sacred quest—
He then departed from the lands grown old.

XL.

To follow far the paths of deadly war—
The strife of Catalonia, fierce Navarre;
To dream by campfires in the Cevennes—
Of home and Hildegrade, of Love and Peace:
"Yet shalt thou meet with Lupo, Roland, when
The Saracen tumults give thee release;
But dark the Pyrenees in every glen,
Be guarded with all care, and cautiously;
Thick woods in ambush may encompass thee:"
This said the King: "shall not be hushed the sea,
Till all his rash affirms of wrath with me

Are well fulfilled,—replete with dastard pain—
Ha! that he dares contend for Acquitaine!
The turbulent, proud, vassal—reckless still—
Rebels, and so must feel my power's will!"

XLI.

Revolt was struggling still in Aquitaine;
Much effort, to the monarch, did remain,
To firmly organize each new-made state,
With judgment without triumph—ne'er elate
Was the great genial King o'er the subdued—
Providing loyal government, and good :
But, while arranging these details, some strife,
Impending on the Saxon north-frontier,
Divided his attention, there and here:
The Saracens collected, ever rife
For tumult's chances; and, not having fear,
Since this dread news had called the King away,
They poured down into Arragon, that day :
'Twas Roland, they attacked; twas Roland met
The terrible onslaught, remembered yet,
Of Saragossa's fierce contested hours—
Thousands of Saracens slain round its towers—
The mist of history, dimly o'er it lowers :
But that great victory of the valliant Franks,
To Roland de Roncevalles, owes equal thanks.

XLII.

Days at Ehrenfels.

Elsewhere, what times of change did intervene
At Ehrenfels? Fair Luidgarde the queen   •
Had come to dwell with her young maiden friend:
They now were three together, with the mother
Of Hildegarde, companions, to the end—
In absence of the husband, friend, or brother—
That separate loneliness might lessened be,
And days of hope, passed uneventfully.
" Issem ! hang helmets on the towers, to-day;
Perchance, some pilgrim, hitherward may stray,
In weariness to rest, with palm and staff ;
Thou art not mindful of their needs, not half!
Look out, and see what rustles through the wood,
Or tramples in the valley !"   Issem stood,
A watchman on the battlements, in vain :
No golden spurs came over field or flood,
No crested helmet glinted on the plain :
Soundless the horn of Issem, every eve,
After the day passed, while she lived to grieve.

XLIII.

"Change watch good Issem, until dawn: and lay
The lights along the ramparts—he may come !
Be not unmindful of who speed this way !"
Issem incredulous, of hope, seemed dumb:
—So speaking, Hildegarde in patient gloom,
Looked from the lofty windows of her room;

And in her voice, once sweetness all there was,
The tone most over-sweet, grown querulous,—
As of a falchion that is quivering thrown
Under the rider while the fight goes on,
Or like the heron's heart, in contest torn,
Beneath the falcon's wing in flight upborne:
Still, at the morn, the watchman's summoned word
Brought no news other than the eve had heard.

XLIV.

"Within the wood, my Lady, there's no stir;
No rider bends the branch, or tramps the bur;
No dust is blown, no feathers of a crest,
Or broidered cuirass of a warrior's breast!"
—Silent she listened, silent—seemed content;
Then slowly, oft not noting where she went,
Musing she walked, with veil and shawl wrapped
    close,
Breathing the wan mists as they slowly rose
Mid transient shadows of soft, heavy bloom,
That made her faithful thoughts see Roland's plume:
Albeit, she did know, engaging thought
Was in the splendor of her fancy wrought:
By rippling stream and beech-wood, she delayed,
Until the evening star soft splendor made:
By Nixa's crystal spring and fairy grot
She passed alone, returning—fearing not:
The light or shadow hovering on the grass,
Might be the sprite of Nixa—dared she pass?
Those childish fancies came not now, alas!
And, O ye stars! if any feet have trod
Upon ye—they were things she said to God.

XLV.

" The gloom of night clings to the morning yet,
Where pearls of dawn amid the shadows met;
So I remember, though he may forget!
Roland, though I should make sweet plaint all
   night,
I could not tell thee all the wrong, the right,
The pain of loving thee, and the delight!
Though I should break my heart till break of day,
What then? what more, my Lord? what shall I
   say?
This is as it should be—and was alway!
I tell thee of the day, not in thy sight!
I tell thee of the night, when it is night!
How many days and nights, like these, take flight:
With unclosed lips, I breathe faint little sighs,
And turn so still—the wall hath no replies!
At last I sleep when wakeful feeling dies!"
—With such soft supplication, into sleep
She passed at last—short slumbers, always deep:
With heavy faintness of what pain had been,
The roseate glow not on her pale cheek seen,
Despite of all prosaic things may prove,
She dared to live, and sigh, and die for Love.

XLVI.

He had not come that day, though now three years
Had canceled hope's reserves, and gathered fears:
Sometimes she wept, or with adjuring thrill,
Implored to weep—restraint weeps not at will: ·
Tears, where are ye? Down in the deep heart's urn,

And coming singly to the lids that burn
With strained anguish.   Oh ! ye have a power—
The peace of a resigned and tender hour !
No Peri ever hailed ye, boon of earth !
With half the longing your forbidden worth
Comes o'er the heart whose proud, rebelling eyes
Would send ye back, all hushed, where bleeding lies
A carven mouth of grief beneath its wing—
The refuge of barbed years—a wounded thing !

XLVII.

He had not come; because a journey then
Meant passing like a dream,—returning, when
The long months filled to years, and the lone seas
Brought dimly back the sails of shattered Peace.
—She feared, but dared not question *what* she
    feared:
Betimes, a herald from the King appeared,
And news from Saxon wars—but, not from him
For whom, her cheek so paled, and eyes grew dim:
Soldiers and pilgrims, by the thousands, went
To those far lands where he had pitched his tent:
—She knew, alas, that hardly half returned
More surely, fondly, truly her heart mourned:
The dust and lustre of wide plains at noon,
Made lingering rest and shade, the traveler's boon;
But the devoted palmer's cloak and stave,
Might find his journey's end, a wayside grave ;
For, in those days, the *plague*, contaminate,
Gave eastern journeyers a hurried fate:
—Expectant love might through such absence wait,

While long the hearts desire, so supplicate,
Could only answered be, with "Oh, too late!"

XLVIII.

There is a mountain shrine—St. Roch's—where
All sylvan grandeurs mingle with sweet prayer,
The beechwood's verdure, and the fount, and thorn
Whose near white blossoms fall on breaths of morn;
All gay luxuriance whose genial breeze
Goes on the sunshine to the distant seas;
The sun's pure deeps of sapphire, and the fold
Of lambs all gather'd, ere its last ray's gold:
—With the rose-folded eyelids of sweet tears,
The beautiful, once only, of the years,—
There, in the midst of those who offered vows,
Knelt Hildegarde with gently shaded brows,
Over her pale hands bended to the rail—
Only, as yet, her golden hair their veil:
—Of late, she whispered secret mournful things,
Touched with redundance of love's hidden springs:
"Lo! the Lamb lieth on the altar's stone,
And I, O God, am here with thee alone!
Can I not love *Thee*, O my God, above?
And thus forget the pain of human love?
But no: the thoughts he shares, mine anguish
    prove!
Sometime, somewhere, beyond the clearest skies,
I hope to see again those dear, deep eyes
Look on me, after life's or death's surprise!"

XLIX.

But we may tell when she had waited long,
For pilgrim's tidings, or for minstrel's song :
—O'er the far solitudes subdued and vast,
At last a day auspicious seemed—at last,
A day ! it may be as an almond wand,
Where, with sweet surprise, a flower is found ;
Or, like Arabian bee that from a rose
Feeds—then with venom, and not honey, goes
To sting to madness, on the Kamsin's wind,
When all the white, hot plains make gazing blind:
—The long untrodden cliffs, two travelers climbed,
When slow, St. Roch's bell for vespers chimed—
Their quiet converse was most earnest toned ;
Its whispered theme, some subtle secret owned.

L.

"You watch her, and sing lays, while I explain,"
This said the younger, "think of Acquitaine,
And let no pity of your soul arise
For wringing hands of hers, or tearful eyes !"
"I know" the other said, "how just is this :
But how malignant too, a *question* is !"
"I am exacting as the king Clovis"[15]
—His comrade answered with a careless laugh—
"Who could not cut the Soissons' vase in half,
And could not have it for his royal share—
To give it back for good St. Remi's prayer :
But when his soldier struck it with an axe,
To make it subject to no more contest,

—The richest thing of booty in the sacks,
Less value then became than all the rest—
.Its beauty, to a battered mass, compressed:
Clovis said naught at what had been done to it,
But sent it back—the prelate scarcely knew it;
But, one year after, levied was its tax:
The soldier in some dicipline was lax—
"Your shield! your armor! spotted all with rust,"
The king roared, as he threw them in the dust:
"*I* strike as *you* struck Soissons' vase that day!
It was wrought silver, and *you* are but clay!"
One blow of the *francisque,* and dead he lay.

LI.

With careless jest and such light anecdote,
They sauntered till they reached the castle's moat;
But this much of their talk displayed an air
Of enterprise, and courage, learning rare—
Not always found in pilgrims given to prayer:
Each shoulder marked, each shell-medallioned hat,[16]
Donned it, the pilgrim's garb, malice like that?
Lo! in each eye, a fierce and dull gray light—
Where sits the condor, bird of haughty flight,
On rugged Andes, beneath Pampas skies —
Such is the spirit that such glance implies:
Under each cloak soft flowing, mailed and strong
Lithe limbs; and, like the Torso studied long,
Carved shoulders of fine mould and massive grace—
These the dread beauties of each form and face:
The gates were reached, a horn's blast sped their call,
And welcome, tendered by the Senechal.

LII.

Effacing trace of trembling, hope and fear,
With glad expectance;—what may she now hear?
So deemed the castle maiden as with haste,
The banquet hall's full laden board, she graced:
Then eyes of furtive guile subdued their glance,
Looked down with semblance mild of pious trance,·
And cautious watchfulness of manner some,
Waiting the questions, that they knew would come,
With answers ready, for love's queries, traced:
Queen Luidgarde, the lady mother—all
Gave gracious welcome in the banquet hall;
And servants went and came with busy call;
For those were men of note, it was assumed,
Though now in pilgrim garb not knightly plumed;
The Duke Friuli and brave Count Gerold,[17]
Whose deeds, with Charlemagne, were true and
  bold
In Hunnish wars of doubtful, hard event:
These lies were told with grace and compliment,
And heard with courteous faith, all confident.

LIII.

Festooned, with mountain boughs of freshest green,
The armor-laden walls were brightly hung;
The shining rings of *hauberks* gleamed between,
In polished splendor, near great chandeliers
Whose lighted waxen-tapers, o'er them flung,
A softened brilliancy like stars or tears—
Though nothing added to ancestral years,
Whose glorious deeds, the bards had often sung,

Of brave old warriors whose steel-armor now
Rested in radiance, under lamp and bough.
—The daring visitants had secret fear ;
For, Issem and his warders were outside ;
But naught of recognition did appear,
Or, had it—*there*, at once, the culprits, died :—
Their journey short to a deserving tomb,—
There leaning, half concealed in the warm gloom
Of the carved, oaken mantel whose great hearth
Threw o'er the festal-board its genial mirth.

LIV.

They watched the ladies waiting on the queen,
With curious eyes of interest—not all holy—
And inconsistent with the melancholy.
Most usual in such men of pilgrim mien :
—There sat fair Hildegarde amidst her maidens;
The one who bore the water for her hands,
And twined her gold brown hair with jeweled
     strands,
Was nearest, chatting, with the softest cadence
Of gladness and sweet hope in her young voice—
They now might hear of Roland, and rejoice :
"Ask him, dear lady, and be not afraid !
No doubt, he knows of Roland, why delayed ?"
This playful importunity obeyed,
What Hildegarde's own wish had not essayed
As yet ; but, waiting till more unobserved
By others—then, her purpose strong, she nerved,
With shy, sweet smiles, responsive to the word
Of her affectionate and faithful friend,

Who knew that Roland's name was like the chord
Where the deep harmonies in music blend.

LV.

One of the pilgrims sung his sweetest lays,
As other troubadours. of love and praise,
That came from Holy Land in after days:
The joyous festival's glad, careless glee
Gave chance of anxious speech to Hildegarde;
And with some effort's cost of dignity,

Inclining gentle head, and smile's award—
Though tremulous a little at the heart—
She summoned him who stood in gloom apart,
And with mild courage said what seemed so hard.

LVI.

"And hast thou come from lands, O pilgrim, where
The lute, and lance, and corselet fall in prayer?
And foremost martyrs fruitless not? while low,
Their deep atoning hearts in torrents flow?
Is the dread crescent in ascendance yet?
And the red, desert sun in triumph set,
Where the unaltered cross hath lowered stood
The share of sorrow, and the price of blood?
And hast thou seen him, severed long from me?
O faithful journeyer, by land and sea!
I called thee pilgrim," here her grave lips' fold
Parted with smiles,—"and thou art Count Gerold?"
This asking, her voice fell more quietly,
While faintest flush of rose came o'er her cheek,
And, downward looking, she then ceased to speak.

LVII.

Adroitly, he evaded her last tone
Of question, as to what name he did own;
None could discover in the roseate dun
Of his cheek's fine mould—Abu Taurus' son:
His mother was a Christian girl, most fair,
Of the Asturias' mild, and balmy air—
For, oft the rival race of Omar, there,
Turned into lovers' wooing—Moslem prayer:
Or, o'er the wild stream of Abbassides,
Were shed, rose leaves of Christian love and
 peace:
—Not wanting in most chivalrous address
This Arab, Frank, did equal rights possess;
So that our Lupo, as his preference ran,
Might be a gallant Christian Frank at times,
Or a descendant of Abderraman—
His whole rights are not stated in these rhymes:
But his own tact and subtlety adjusted
The role that just then he had to enact;
And Hildegarde confidingly entrusted,
Hope, credulous, to an illiterate fact—
As he responded, with the mildest grace,
Apparent in each act of form and face:

LVIII.

" Lady, the King's knight, Roland, I have seen,
Last—in the towers of Capitoline:
We two oft watched at night, when stars grew
 pale,
The fire-flies on the slopes of Arno's vale;

And listened to the dulcet, chirping hums,
Or mystic movements—strange unceasing thrums
Of the Cicada, in the barley-blooms ;
Where the dark olive and the bright pale vine,
Luxuriant, alternate, intertwine.
The classic mantles of Romaic tombs !
Far he had come, his valliant mission through,
Successful from where clouds of Syrian blue,
O'er mount and plain of journey, warmly soar;
When, at the Tiber's mouth, a rested oar
Brought him late orders for a lengthened stay :—
Of accusations made against Leo—
The King would come to Rome, the cause to know;
And might need Roland's aid to strongly show
Impartial judgment to his friend, the Pope :
Who vainly, with conspiracy, did cope !
Stern but devoted, was the calm dismay
Of the Knight, Roland, at this new delay !"

LIX.

"I know," she whispered, "and a holier tie
His pain and peril thus doth sanctify—
To live for me as for his honor die !"
But this to her own heart whose subdued sigh
Gave little outward sign's anxiety.
"Stern but devoted," he continued, "now
Be strong, O lady, I must tell thee how
Not with a vanquished Eagle he would come
Back to the hamlets of his mountain home !"
"Be strong ?   Oh yes: for I have chastened well,
Erewhile my heart's surmises—thou may'st tell

The unfaltering deed—if, with royal right,
He died—then, *I have liv3d*, as infinite !"
"Yea: but I fear the words that may appall
Thee into dark despair, if I recall !
Against Campulus and the base Paschal,
His active part was but disaster all;
And good Pope Leo, from conspiring strife,
Was only saved at cost of Roland's life—
Alas ! thou hearest this, his promised wife !"

LX.

Let not repeatings of the guileful speech
Through all her anguish its whole meanings reach:
There was a quick commotion—sudden fright;
And joy turned to dismay—the deathly blight
Of consternation; hushed was every tongue;
On inquiry expectant, each breath hung
For a few moments : white and still and cold,
She had swooned in deep woe— life's chords
    unstrung :
Cold as the stream, stricken at icy fold,
Of some great avalanche whose thundering swell,
From the high mount into the valley, fell,
And white as that lost wing that, at the gate
Of Heaven, was vanquished—ere it flew to Hell—
After whose whiteness, Death's blackness might
    wait—
The ensign-bearer of dread Azrael !
Dear Hildegarde had heard what Lupo told—
Lupo, the crafty, heartless Lupo, bold :
Oh, not in vain thy Roland's warning, meant

To shield thy trustful heart so innocent!
Alas, alas! in some far, fluttering tent,
Or in the strife of some contested field,
That voice of warning and that "veiled shield!"

LXI.

From morn till midnight, tolled the castle bell!
From midnight until morn, its muffled knell
Resounded sad, grief's tidings far to tell!
And hollow grew the softly rounded cheek;
And pallid blue, the lips that did not speak
For many a weary day and weary week:
—Her constant friend, the faithful Luidgarde,
The king's own wife —all majesty, yet meek—
Watched, by the bedside of her tender ward,
Till—as the sunrise, through the dawn's dim streak,
Faintly perceptible at last appears—
Life's consciousness came back with reason's tears,
The mild safe sea that, ships of sorrow, bears
Into the port of resignation—even
When storms shroud earth and sky—that port is
     heaven!
Tears, tears! yea, tears: else it were madness then
To know that Roland ne'er would come again:
"I fear she'll die" one said unto the other—
The friend so loving, the more loving mother—
And cautious were they, that no word was said
To wake the pain so dear—the pain so dead.

LXII.

Events at Rome.

Though not *all* truth what Lupo's craft did say,
Roland *was* at Rome, that recorded day :
The shrines were robed, for it was blessed May:
In all the bannered streets, the populace
Rode in dense splendor; 'twas a day of grace:
The " Greater Litany's " sweet, solemn close,
By many chorists chanted, grandly rose!
Past St. Sylvester's the long line, and past
St. Stephen's—chorists—banners—Leo last:
From burning censer, floating silver cloud ;
The knee was bent, the reverent head was bowed;
In prayer and hymn, was Jesus' holy name:
Then the chief Pontiff turned, and raised his hand—
Tranquil in blessing or in mild command,
Which, was never known—through the line there
    came,
In hurried breaths and flashing eyes of flame,
Wild cries of blood—a panic seizing all !
Loud voices called, Campulus and Paschal ! [18]

LXIII.

These very men, placed nearest to the side
Of Leo's august state, who yet defied
His solemn and just right, had—that same morn,
Irrelevant, concealing plots of scorn,
And waiting, chances future hours might own—
Accepted marks of signal favor shown,

And with such friendly tact, and consummate,
That Leo still suspected not his fate;
But, in that moment when his hand was lifted,
And that such call of voices loudly rose,—
To scattered tumult the long line was drifted;
And he, at once encompassed by his foes.

LXIV.

Turbulent, traversing each open space,
Did lances' streamers flash, and interlace!
Hatred had slumbered, but it was not dead,
On unsuspecting kindness it had fed:
Too trusting Leo! Close—insatiate,
Arose the deadly cries,—"Down! Mutilate!"
—With coward, trembling hands—for crime is fear,
They bore him prostrate: "Hold, ye dastards!
     Hear!"
Roland's that voice;—they halt to hear him speak,
The glow of his quick wrath hath dyed his cheek!
" Ye that with sacrilege would quench the light
In those pale, bleeding brows, defend your right!
I come, conspirators! Vengeful, I come!
Say, are those pallid lips forever dumb?
Those mute, mild lips that called you Brothers,
     long?
There in the dust, low lying, for your wrong!"

LXV,

Scene that was terrible! Men desperate!
They dared not stop, sheathed in the heart of hate;
A moment, and the glimmering dust arose

With ring of helmets and with javelin blows :
There Roland's violet mantle, floating high,
Cleaved a free pathway where the foremost die.
"Match ye with this," he cried, "your plots of
    harm !"
And fast and true, fell his descending arm ;
As tremor of faint stars o'er fallen snow,
Shuddered the jeweled helmet on his brow,
So damp with ardor's haste—so pale with zeal,
Appalling triumph !—this didst thou reveal.

LXVI.

The almost lifeless Leo then was borne
To St. Erasmus;—all the night till morn,
Each gallant enemy, and zealous friend,
Watched, holding counsel,—life and death impend,
Though he should be a prisoner, if his life
Were spared for further question in the strife :
Meanwhile, within the monastery, were found
Adherents whose devotion was sincere—
His chamberlain, Albinus, closer bound
This strong co-operative aid; though fear
Imbued his every movement, not untried
He left each means—and enmity defied :.
Down from the walls, in safety to the ground,
They lowered Leo at the dead of night,
When scarce recovered from his dangerous wound,
—And ere his enemies perceived his flight :
Before three days had passed, the King had come
With speed—encamping near the walls of Rome;
There Roland's tendered sword, the first glad gift,

That charmed his smiling eyes, whose upward lift
At lighted altars, o'er that sword austere,—
Yea, wept—in hallowed love, in pride and fear !

LXVII.

The Convent of Nonnenwerth.

Return, where never changed, the mists that hung
Moving like censers that are softly swung
Upon the mountains, or like robes and feet
That, it was said, are beautiful to meet—
Where Hildegarde, with white enfolded hands
That on her lap were resting—and blue bands
Of silken ribbon on her tresses shining,
And head, upon her bosom, half inclining:
Thinking of Roland and, perhaps, repining—
Traversed, in thought, the scenes of distant lands:
—Wholly endowed with contemplation's sense,
She felt that love was prayer ; in her soul's deep,
Prayer and holy love a tryst did keep—
A rapt resolve of some new thought intense.

LXVIII.

Dark was her soul; but, like the falcon's flight,
That rises startled from the dews of night—
Assuaging fear with lofty thoughts, like stars
That set before the hour of dawn unbars
The day unto the night.   Rainbow and cloud !
In all life's storms, ye are not disallowed !
Though hope be all discrowned, and time not life,
Within the haunted breast, ye meet the strife !

When man's heart is a shoreless, soundless deep,
What floating flowers unfold and o'er it sweep,
On, tideward to the cliffs of some rock-tomb
That stirs not though the billows toss in gloom,
Glancing, like quickened pain, against the foam
Whose desolation shines beneath thy dome!
As one such flower, along life's tide she swept—
Saddest of all things on that path of dread,
—Against the billows' strength, vain conflict kept;
For, still a thousand tears her dear eyes wept,
And low unlifted her love-mourning head:
Still where was thrown the shadow of the past,
Her heart reached high a flame-enwreathed mast,
Whose sails were burning and whose bays seemed
    fire,
—The sight of shore to the wrecked hope's desire.
Proverbial love!—thou 'rt known by many names;
But thou didst come to her, with these thy claims,
In dreamlike harmony that had become,
Her full heart's patience, as with laden hum,
On slumbrous summer-winds, the voyager
Starts from the troubled rose, with wings astir.

LXIX.

"Thy place of sanctity, O Nonnenwerth!
Is now the chosen, peaceful spot on earth
Where I can bear to live," she musing said:
"Oh, I shall bind my brows, as one lain dead,
Where thy majestic bells, at eventide,
Along the waters of the pure lake glide!
Roland! Roland! thy chimes will seem to call,

—Sentence and prophecy, I will understand!
Roland! Roland! answering not at all—
From o'er the sea nor o'er the mountain land!
But, like the watched dove, I will lift my thought,
Far out of sad realms that on earth are sought!
Eternal purpose! serene to be fulfilled,
Forever irrevocable, strongly willed,
Nothing to expiate—sacrifice alone—
Love's truest offering when its will is done!''

LXX.

And here love's pain and tenderness, once more,
The balmy murmur of deep grief, did pour;
And well it was; for, as by Euphrates,
They sat and sighed for days forever flown—
Patience rose softly on the plumes of peace,
With songs of the true heart's harmonious moan,
—The sorrow bravely borne, this sign, shall own:
"Let not the Lyre sleep," unto them was said;—
They answered, looking up with eyes that plead,
''Oh yes! unto our sorrow, we shall sing!
There is, perhaps, some drop, ye did not bring,
That had made overfull our misery,
And given to mourners the sad right to die!''
How great, then, is the grief that doth deny
The last, blest peace of death—the final sigh:
This death in life was hers—like the Sybil,
—To live and to remember fondly still:
Such song of consolation, such unrest—
Inheritance—forever, in her breast.

· LXXI.

"The sentence *I have loved*—alas, alas!
What end of anything shall come to pass?
What bloom, what blossom dieth as the grass?
 Beneath my feet are those things—now, my love
Doth lead my. heart, and lift my eyes above!
But oft I know my thoughts will darkly brood,
Like shadows in the cedars of the wood,
Thy soul within them, Roland! and thy name
Within them, ashes left when quenched the flame!.
There shalt thou walk upon the slumbrous sea,
Thy power through darkness still sustaining me—
The storm—the waves—the night of Galilee!
It shall be known—the darkness, fear, and pain—
Known that I watched for thee across the main,
And that my head upon thy feet hath lain!
Dark are the Olives now, my love and lord!
And near my lips, the chalice and the word
That Jesus uttered when the angel heard!
Dark are the Olives, and I too afraid,
As when the chalice to his lips was laid ;
And I too, list to what the angel said!
I list to what the angel said—for thou
Mayst no word say to me! Roland, no sign
From thee! I lie, as one at day's decline
May lie, in shadow of grief's mountain brow!
Many a watch, like last night's watch, I'll keep
When the soft seals do not fall into sleep,
While lying—dying—loving thee—I'll weep!
—Angel of record! take some note of this!
Come down to me, through darkness, with the kiss

" All the dreamy day in cymar of gold,
  The Lurly maiden sits where cliffs are cold ;
  Swiftly her white hands in the sunset shine,
  With gleaming golden comb and tresses fine."

Page 149.—Stanza XIX.

In dreams, somehow, of his sweet passion's bliss!
Or bear me through the realms of earth and air,
Unconscious of my waking woe's despair,
And lay me in his sleeping bosom fair—
There would I be with him at rest, somewhere!
—Impenetrable God! what do I say?
My life to thee—one consecrated day!
Feeling and thought of mine, Thy will shall sway!"

LXXII.

The basement, Gothic arches, and facade
Of Nonnenwerth to-day are not much changed,
Although in dreadful wars, 'twas often made
The scene where ruthless footsteps careless ranged,
—It served as a hotel or hospital:
The sanctity of custom might recall
In vain old usage—or its shelter fall
Upon the soldier doomed to couch and pall;
And we may thus suppose that many a scar,
Together with the ravages of time,
Hath marked its walls, in peace as well as war,
—A renovated ruin—old—sublime!
In that past, ancient day, 'twas thus arrayed:
Within the chapel, richly overlaid
And gilded the high altar's balustrade:
The painted ceiling and sacristy door,
With decorative art, all covered o'er:
Bright leaves and cornices—no open space
Not covered by the frescos of the walls:
Sts. Peter and Lorenzo—each saint's face
A work of art by some hand o'er which falls

The veil of nameless time—though sometimes fair,
Those frescos old are valued more as rare
Old relics of the early Christian art—
Such as St. John, St. Paul, the Sacred Heart—
Before the Renaissance did softly part
The folds of drapery that hid the morn
Of splendor, that its birth came to adorn.

LXXIII.

Many of those old pictures were on plate
Of gold and silver—all backgrounds of gilt—
Though sometimes upon wood, with frames ornate
Of silver, set with jewels, as though spilt
In rich confusion; on the frame's bright marge,
Were precious stones of all kinds—often large:
Those paintings, mostly Greek, and whether wood
Or plate, the outlines always hard and rude,
—In size not larger than a foot or two—
Said to be painted by St. Luke—if true,
They were entitled to their dingy hue;
But some old frescos were of size immense,
And quite appalling to the startled sense:
The artists, evidently, used more skill
To portray satan's power of evil will,
Than to exemplify the angels—all
The latter were left out, or made quite small.

LXXIV.

But the chief devil, always very big,
Was made the hero of the awful scene,
Gnawing sinners, and caring not a fig

While he devoured them, whether fat or lean :
His teeth were marvellously long—his mouth
Would serve a " carpet-bagger" going South,
Its powers of capacity so great ;
But judging the expression on his face,
He did not relish much the food he ate,
—No doubt, disgusted with the sinful race—
Though sternly, he fulfilled each victim's fate,
While standing to his middle in a pool
Made red to simulate the fiercest fire :
Alas ! Beholding this, is man a fool
To give his heart up to each base desire ?
No wonder, the old Saints' ascetic rule
Made them be painted, on the wall, up higher,
— A row of holy men, upon a bench,
To which no imp or devil could aspire—
And, on the burning lake that naught could quench,
They looked, in grave solemnity, as though,
Were it not for the honor of the thing,
They'd rather be disporting there below,
Where many little sinners, wild did fling
Themselves about in various attitudes :
An angel, at one side, carefully weighed
A few good-sized ones, in a pair of scales,
—Appearing sad in judgment, and dismayed
At how preponderance of sin prevails—
These were presented, in the interludes
Of Satan's feasting, as the last new goods.

LXXV.

The fresco, as described, herein above,
Was painted, under a descending dove,

In Nonnenwerth's large porch, so high and wide—
It nearly covered all the space, one side:
'Twas given the convent by Costanz Cloro
Whose wife became a convert first, then he,
—They lived before Van Rhyn or Da Vinci;
And 'twas not painted by Fiamingo,
Or even Cimabue, or Albert Durer,
—For they lived after, though so long ago—
Its gifted artist's name, no records show;
And speculation cannot make us surer,—
Nor could it, then, have been by Tintoretto :
Such awful names have all this artist set—oh,
It would distract one, the whole list, to tell—
—Tibaldi, Vasari and Raffaelle—
I might continue, and their number swell—
But since I name not this one, let them go—
His name's the one I don't exactly know.

LXXVI.

The convent was not always Ursuline—
Brendaine, perh'aps—if not, Benedettine;
The early annalists only combine,
To give accounts distinct and separate—
Its orders had, each one, unequal date :
But, in those days, the nuns wore cloth of fine
White texture, as a flowing tunic made
In manner as a sash—the head o'erlaid
With a Greek band of modest ornament:
O'er Longobardo books of ritual,
At prayer and service, their mild eyes were bent;
And all were ladies of the noblest birth

Who were admitted nuns at Nonnenwerth :
The long sleeves of the robes were made to fall,
A covering to soft bands of fairest grace;
And the Greek band, or forehead's broidered pall,
Was palely beautiful above each face:
—If one should go at noon or eventide
To sit within the chapel—there beside
The coro railings—white, as if they died,
And there were statuesque and kneeling still,
—The silence broken only by the thrill
Of the sweet chant, half prayer, half hymn, they
 made—
Some of them always in that sacred place,
Though all the church besides were empty space,
Or nearly so: perceiving this, afraid,   •
Almost, would be beholders, at the scene
So purely passive, pallid, and serene—
Those kneeling nuns, behind the coro's screen.

LXXVII.

Among them there was one who was yet young,
Of all the coro nuns, she sweetest sung;
And oft sent messages to Hildegarde,
After the service, through the coro barred:
They had been fond companions in the days
Of childhood's happy studies and glad plays;
And Angiola, this was her sweet name,
Grieved for the grief that on her fair friend came:
" Be one of us," she said, "and bear thy loss !
They too shall wear the crown who wear the
 cross ! "

It needed little of such influence—
Already had the world-resigning sense
Come over Hildegarde conclusively—
The place, its custom, and its novelty,
Claimed her attention—which she went to see ·
Walking the corriders beside her friend—
The other nuns, that met them, light did bend
Each gentle head with smiles of mild salute
And welcome, low-voiced as a Dorian flute.

LXXVIII.

While pleased with all she saw, through spacious
    halls,
Refectory, and Dormitorio,
The church, the gardens—till the sunset glow
Sank o'er the willow marge, and o'er the flow
Of river-tide—these earnest friends did go :
—After the entrance, a commodious stair
Led to the topmost chambers, and the tower
Whose spire reached upward through ethereal air,
O'er grounds of willow bloom, and garden flower,
And clear, bright windows, that looked on the
    Rhine,
Whose distant, trellised hillsides of pale green
Nurtured the amethystic jeweled vine,
While the blue winding river flowed between,
Dimly far onward—beautifully grand!
The Rhine, the Rhine of that fair mountain land!
Here might she dwell henceforth in blissful peace,
Apart from life, to give time's woe surcease ;
And then she named a certain day of choice,

When she would, soon return, all this to share :
Her resolution made the nuns rejoice—
The beat of the simandro called to prayer—
Her visit she delayed, to join them there.

LXXIX.

Soon after, she returned to Ehrenfels,
To make avowal of her new intent:
That day a message to the castle sent,
With kingly retinue and herald bells,
Informed the queen—his majesty the king
Would wait for her, at Tours, that they would
  bring
Her court and ladies, while he waited there :
—At this time Luidgarde would go to Tours,
To seek some blessed waters' shrine of cure;
The dread disease that, after caused her death,
Was then oppressing her—with faint, quick breath,
She welcomed Hildegarde's return, and then,
With courteous care, disposed the kingly men
To banquet; and, preparing to depart,
She pressed her friend, in fervor, to her heart:
—"Lord give thee peace, my dear," she said,
  "I go;
With me life seems to fade; and yet, on me,
The fondest kingly love, its joys bestow—
See how life's strange allotments seem to be !
Abide then in God's will, we cannot see
What may be best for us—what is grief's right ?
One flower struck at the root, one left to bloom,

Must each have after-part of equal blight,
And may have bloomed and blossomed on a tomb!"

LXXX.

And then they spoke of many other things—
Their friendship was like Iris' rainbow wings,
Or like the shield of Pallas, tried and true,
The sympathies so varied of these two,
And yet into one bow so lightly hung;
For gentle Luidgarde was also young,
And very dear unto her kingly lord—
This, tenderly expressed his message word—
At that same hour, his heart with woe was wrung,
In fear of the impending loss of her,
And he had called physicians to confer
About her state of health.   She now proposed
That both the ladies go with her to Tours,
In order, that no circumstance abjure
Their bond of sweet companionship—disclosed
Must be the plan of Hildegarde, so late,
Made the intention of her future fate.

LXXXI.

That moment, Lady Heligoland came
Into the queen's apartment—she, the same
Mentioned as mother of our heroine,
And eldest sister of the lovely queen :
—"I will go with you, dear, she kindly said,
And preparation shall at once be made!"
Then, turning to her daughter, she perceived
That with some hesitating thought, she grieved :

—" Dear mother, loneliness will be, 'tis true,
As though thy rose of love, bereft of dew,
Missed, for the time, the sunshine that it knew!"
Then on her mother's bosom she did lean—
"If I go not with thee and with the queen,
I can have favored time to try the vow
In the white veil"—here bending her head low—
"I wish to go to Nonnenwerth, you know!"
—"My dear, as you decide, it shall be so,
And with my blessing, I will let thee go!
Yet, dear, with some reluctance, this I say—
I will try not to miss thee while away:
My journey with the queen will then be good,
Since I will not be here in solitude!"

LXXXII.

Days passed, and, in one short week from that day,
Where shadows darkled from the sun's bright ray,
There was a festa in the forest trees,
A festa of farewell by Hildegarde:
The village maidens gathered all around;
And after morn's and noon's festivities,
She took them to the castle court, or yard,
And dropping from the windows to the ground
Her silken robes and laces—did award
To each and all of them, some present fair—
Dividing equally, each share and share:
Pleased, they received them, but less pleased the
    word
That they received with them of sad farewell—
Some little sobs and tears there softly fell:

*13

Each one, in turn, came near and kissed her cheek,
While with full heart she stood, and did not speak :
These were the maidens that with roundelay,
When Roland was a boy—she, queen of May—
At the *rosalia*, laid the garland-rose
Upon her girlish brow's pure, bright repose.

LXXXIII.

The next morn, all three ladies would take leave
Of Ehrenfels, though parting's last reprieve
With Hildegarde might be deferred a day—
They would, at Nonnenwerth, make some delay,
Attending while bestowed was her white veil—
By route of journey it was on their way,
A journey beautiful o'er hill and dale.
The knights of escort waited in the glade,
With varied plumes and sashes, bright arrayed,
And pages held the stirrups, while they mounted ;
—They rode on horses, in a cavalcade,
—Fifty knights-at-arms, in all, when counted:
But when the drawbridge fell, and Hildegarde
Lingering the last one, ere she passed beyond,
With foot upon the stirrup, thought how hard
To part with childhood's things, associate, fond,
She stopped to give them one, last, farewell glance,
And bear them still onward in remembrance.

LXXXIV.

Her bower-window, whose Eolian chord
To the spring zephyr made responsive thrill,
The woodland park, the stream and rocky ford,

The softness of the sunrise on the hill,
And the low murmur of the distant mill:
—Absorbed she gazed, when sudden, the old ward,
With hand upon the bridle rein, stood near
In deprecating tenderness—half fear:
—"My Lady, have I looked so long in vain,
That thou wilt never view these towers again,
That were my posts of watch?" As the tide
  strands
Reluctant yield their bright waves to the sea,
He seemed o'erwhelmed with his strong agony;
Kneeling, he clasped her robe, between his hands,
Tightly, and to his lips he lifted it:—
"In my old age, so desolate, I'll sit
To see thy face no more—thy face no more!"
At thought of this, convulsive bending o'er
The hands he pressed, restrainless grew his woe,
As the red star of tempest on the flow
Of midnight waters in the gloom below:
As he had watched for her o'er mountain lands,
Her wishes, to affection, were commands;
Oft he had borne her o'er the torrent sands,
To keep her delicate, small feet from damp;
And when she was afraid, as children are
When twilight fades, and rises the night-star,
'Twas always Issem that had borne the lamp.

LXXXV.

She laid her hand upon his aged head,
"Weep not, O Issem," she then sadly said:
"I go where in the choir's sweet melodies,

Thy lute songs of old time will softly rise!
Issem, I too, feel quiver in mine eyes,
The tears of kind remembrance, and now there
I see myself a child with clustering hair,
The spring's breath free upon a sunny brow,
And mildly, as I bless thine aged one now!
Thy hand light as a fawn's foot, e'er to mark
The opening flower, the path of upward lark—
These things shall still go with me to a shrine
Of undimmed beauty, as devout as thine!"
Then covering her eyes, she said no more;
But hastening, joined those who had gone before.

LXXXVI.

Departing, all were on the journey then—
Along the river side, by rock and glen,
Till reaching Nonnenwerth, they had such rest
As glad reception gave the welcome guest—
The escort-knights and queenly court were made
Encampments in the ground of willow shade,
Finding not room for all within the walls:
—The chapel, hung with ivy coronals,
All was made ready for the lofty theme
Of praise and sacrifice—the altar's gleam
Burned with soft luster—the attending train
Of sweet-voiced nuns upraised a soft refrain,
And friends were gathered, and a solemn Mass
Was chanted, while in order they did pass
Around the rail to gather at her side,
When she avowed herself the white Christ-bride,
That mystic hour accepted and denied:—

Her hair was garlanded—each separate tress
Of seven tresses, touched upon the end
With melted wax: a box, that held the dress
Of white, was brought—then kneeling, she did
   bend,
The robe was given to the priest to bless—
The abbess cut the tresses, one by one,
And placed the white veil on her—all was done.

LXXXVII.

After, the glad acclaims of welcome made,
The day was passed with the rejoicing guests;
And all the other nuns, vieing, essayed
To show the rose-bloom of the soul, that rests
Longest upon religious eminence;
Imagination that becomes intense,
And finer, the perception of each sense—
The violent contrasts of solitude:
—The mind, reliant on itself, imbued
With efforts, purposes—all vainly strewed
Beside the green shore and the current's lave,
Mid roses wild that grew upon a grave,
Accepts what hope presents. and calls it good,
Because, but partially, 'tis understood—
For, knowing things too well, we are not pleased,
Nothing on earth will satisfy the heart;
Here is the secret of the thought released,
To seek, beyond the earth, the better part.

LXXXVIII.

There was one thing that happened very strange,
—Just at the moment when she bowed her head,

And that bestowal of the veil was made,
The abbess then reached forward to exchange,
With Hildegarde, the taper that she held—
When lo! as though by unseen hands, 'twas
    felled—
It dropped and quenched, its swiftly passing flame
Catching her veil a moment—quickly red
Her lambent cheek, as the bright flame that fled,
And soon, as whitely paled, as one just dead:
—Newly asleep that night in a strange place,
Her dreams were troubled—one familiar face
Haunted her memory, and she waked, and heard
A low, soft bell that on the midnight stirred;
Then, waking her companion from repose,
She asked the meaning of the deep'ning tone—
Who, trembling as in fear, or one alone,
Crossing herself, proceeded to disclose
To Hildegarde the meaning of the bell.
—" San Benedetto, sister dear, would tell
How pleased he is upon the choice you've made!"
And yet, she shuddered still as one afraid—
There was a custom of the olden time,
San Benedetto tolled a midnight chime
Of deep, unearthly sweetness, whene'er one
Was added to the convent—a white nun:
This was to tell her that his great desire
Was her continuance of purpose high—
From the first trial, that she still aspire,
And lift her hopes, to Immortality.

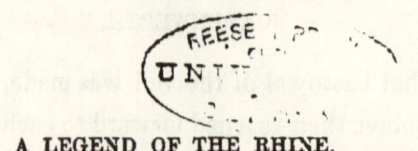
LXXXIX.

Thus letting her fond heart fold in its blight—
Ah me ! the fleeting months whose veil was white,
Testing the soul that might not choose aright:
What sorrow had she missed ?—What destiny ?
The prayers of yielding hopes' surrendered will,
No tender, last reprieve did them delight—
The changeful future, who can e'er foresee:
Hushed, every strong unrest's repining thrill,
Only the curving lines grew quivering deep,
Where citadels of feeling softly sleep,
On the lip's pure rose — the brow's Madonna
    grace—
With all that heaven may seek, and earth efface.
A year's novitiate of such peaceful balm,
The past now dead to her—the future blank—
The final vows, could they bring deeper calm?
Or, were they like a towering cloud's dark bank ?

XC.

When formed a purpose, we may never know
What may the sequel of its future show:
—As the deep " Cherr! Cherr!" of the honey-guide
That leads to shadows of the mountain side,
Where, following, is found the bees' full comb
If still unwearied will the hunter roam:
But, for all that O wanderer, beware !
The honey-guide may, with the self-same care,
Lead those who follow into bush or snare,
The sleeping tiger's, or the lion's lair,

Or to the under-growth whose cobra hides,
And where the stealthy panther's footstep glides:
The day came of the last decisive "yes,"
"What is thy purpose?" asked those whom she
  met,
"Or hath the year brought unto thee regret?"
She shook her head and smiled: they answered,
  "Bless
Thee, sister dear! and may thy hopes be true,
And sweet as precious frankincense whose dew
The desert sands have gathered through the night,
And yet, behold! it bloometh at the light,
And in the blazing heat of the noon-tide,
It does not perish, trampling hoofs shed wide
Its soft, rich perfume on the desert air,
Imperishable ever, it is there.

XCI.

Again the church was filled; invited guests
Crowded the portico; and rich bequests
Were given; and the grand, pontifical,
High Mass was chanted by a cardinal:
A sheet of parchment, with gilt arabesque,
The oath of formula, lay on the desk;
And on the floor was a black carpet, spread—
Prostrate upon it, on her face she lay:
A funeral-cloth thrown o'er from foot to head,
Upon it neither flower nor fragrant spray,
But in the center was, embroidered white,
A human skull, betwen the torches' light
That burned at the four corners; while a bell,

With muffled cadence on the wind's deep swell
Was tolled, the cardinal her thus conjured
With hope immortal, beyond earth, assured:
" O thou who sleepest in cold death, awake!
God will enlighten thee, for his own sake!"

XCII.

At the first invocation, the nuns drew
The black cloth off; and, at the second, she
Arose upon the carpet, on one knee:
Again one light went out—a sharp wind blew
Into a doorway opened—some, that knew
The cause of her resolve, made strange remark,
How omen-like it was, the taper dark
A second time—" Come back, appear, reply,"
It surely asked against her destiny:
As it was newly lighted, so sublime
It gleamed, a signal of the future time:
At the third call, arising to her feet—
The abbess, with the black veil, came to meet
Her—then she signed the oath of formula,
While all was breathless—silence, and hushed awe:
And, robing o'er her tunic the black veil,
Her pale, fair face seemed more serenely pale,
—She was enveloped in life's somber pall,
And bound by final vows, without recall.

XCIII.

Hildegarde was now a devoted nun,
Her life on earth and Roland's death were one
In her absorbing thought; her patient heart

Sped to eternal hope, after a time :—
First bends the yielding bow wherefrom the dart
Seeks upward flight and far—the chapel chime
Found her, each morning, midst the lovely throng,
Going through garden-path and corridor;
The while, she smiling, looked up to the strong,
Bright castle of her father, watching for
The loving parents who had come to dwell
In sight of her, for greeting, or farewell:
At morn and eve, her brightly waving hand,
They might seek out from all, and understand
As we in days of God—a thousand years,
From that time unto this, may see her tears:
Martyr and advocate! behold, tis well,
Protest and supplication thou mayst tell!

XCIV.

Return of Roland.

Meanwhile, on Saxon borders, Roland stayed,
But now, alas! too long, too long delayed;
For, sometimes in Arragon or Navarre,
Swift was his post changed, with revolting war,
To this place and to that, of battles din—
Incursions, devastating—also, wherein
The Saxons were aggressive, while the Franks,
In fierce retaliation, sought the banks
Of all their boundary rivers, to repress—
Holding dominions, by each strong fortress,
Till permanent subjection, at his feet,

Made, everywhere, each strong success complete
To Charlemagne, whose measures were defense,
And not ambition—violated sense
Of barbarous craft on part of Wittikind,
Who robbed, and who destroyed—who did not
    bind
Himself with honor's pledge that had been given,
Though profuse to submission mean, when driven,
—But winter's barriers of ice and snow,
Made each, in interval, his plans forego :
Then weary, homeward, Roland turned, at last,
When coldest blight had reached the innocence
Of the love, watching long, that called him thence;
Many a peril, he had risked, and passed—
His banner heavy, with a shadowed world,
Soon in his ancient halls it might be furled.

XCV.

Alas! the return, along the peopled shore,
Of Roland—the welcome he would meet no more!
Alas! the day that, on the breeze was borne,
The blast rung sweet and loud from one clear horn,
When maidens, singing, had with garlands come:—
But why, too, were tears?—why were stern lips
    dumb?
Issem, whose answers low, were sad, and brief,
Told the strange story to his stricken chief:
How can the deadly dread that words control,
Make molten barrenness of life's one goal?
Like a staute, beside his steed he stood,
And felt, had he died, ere that hour, 'twere good;

Then low drooped on the sable mane, like lead,
All the utter strength of his proud, young head;
Oh, let us not ask if *she* ever knew
How truly he lived, and how fondly true.

XCVI.

There was feast at the board, and welcoming,
With the bards, the guests, and the noble king;
—But for one who had wandered out alone,
A minstrel chanted this solemn, sweet tone:—

The Minstrel's Chant.

Never on earth!
Never on earth!
To meet any more, but to live apart,
Each passing day, like a veil o'er the heart!
Oh, never to feel the exquisite soul,
Like the bird set free to its wingward goal!

Never on earth!
Never on earth!
Though the light go out of the West each day,
Full of harvested hours—the season's May,
Coming and going, a cycle between,
Dividing sad hearts and that which has been!

Might it be yet?
Oh, vain regret!
The change of a bitterness turning sweet,
A life with its greatest crown at your feet—
Might your dear hands fall in their own loved way,
Ah! those lips are dumb, and those still eyes say:—

We live as dead!
Joy's roses fled!
But, dear, though there never may come replies,
To the faithful heart, wearing only sighs,
Still twilight shall fall into purple haze,
And mornings shall long fill their golden days!

Forgetting not!
What e'er life's lot!
Though forever far, beyond portals pale,
Are the sworn abiding, and sweet avail!
Until death shall come where hope hath striven,
Love will live on, until blest in heaven!

Forget me not!
Forget me not!
When the dust is over the brave, bright brow,
As the blight is over thy fond, sweet vow!
Ah! thy footstep, bruising the green-sward bed,
Shall not waken my veiled and slumbering head!

XCVII.

With the burning stars and his lonely mood,
The singer then left him—well understood—
Pain's thought was as strong as a chainless flood;
Roland hid and wept in the underwood:
—Honors were vain that the faithful king
On him lavished—affections offering—
All the crowns, his renowned young years should
    bring,
Were truly the ashes of roses now—
They might coldly fade on his lonely brow;

For he turned once more from his mountain home,
And journeyed to pray at the shrine of Rome,
And knelt at the feet of the friendly Pope:—
" O Father, displace from me this great woe!
Let the life, I saved, give me love's one hope!
Or, let me but wish the assassin's blow
At thy feet, had laid me, never to know
Refusal, thy clemency may not show!

XCVIII.

" They said she is given to God, my son!
To God—be content—let his will be done!
—Nay, for we cannot—*since the veil is black!*"
So, disconsolate then, he journeyed back,
—If his skiff went ever across the Rhine,
If he dared to seek her with word or sign,
If he dared to ask of her own heart's moan—
Of all this—now, there is little known:
Love's lore is lost in a thousand years,
But the cost is kept of its faithful tears;
Yea, sometimes, a little, as it appears:
And though these are of things not now known
    well—
Yet the vague, dim hints of tradition tell
That for years, alone, in Rolandseck tower,
He lived, letting wither life's love in flower.

XCIX.

What more or less of it—records state
That Roland would watch in his window-chair
From his castle, o'erlooking the convent, where

He had built the towers still standing there,
Till the sunset fell to the evening late,
Strict abnegation—Oh yes! it were well—
But well he loved her, and love would rebel:
—When the glow of the gloom and the dusk fell, oft
Up and down the Rhine went his oar's dip soft;
In the garden path, she might just delay—
He should see her, though no word he might say;
And he often watched till the dawn of day.

C.

One day she was missed, and he heard the bell,
O'er willows and waves, a requiem swell—
'Twas thought that he died in his chair, with pain
Of his stricken heart, but he roused again,
To go back to the wars, and drown his woe
In the crimson tide of the battle flow,
To perish, to ask of the grave its rest,
Midst the conquering brave, foremost and best;
—How he lived and loved, how he died we know;
How he sought the end in the Pyrenees,
While careless of all life's immunities,
And glad to seek death from the grief of life,
Yea, glad to seek death on the fields of strife:
"Once more, once more!" pealed his trumpet's
    clear call,
"Come now gallant knights! Come to Roncevalles!
Let me find thee, O death, somewhere, someway!
Farewell, Rolandseck! fare thee well, to-day!
She is dead, my beautiful! She is clay!"

CI.

With still undying love of liberty,
Treacherous Lupo, Duke of Gascony,
Submitting tribute unto Charlemagne,
Had all this while been suffered to retain
His Duchy in the Pyrenees—so slight,
Under the Crown of France, must tenure be :
Its fastness in the mountains, near the sea,
Gave it position and ancestral right—
Conceding little to contending might :
Only when armies made obedience sure,
The king's authority became secure ;
But Lupo's fierce ambition still denied
To Charlemagne the mountain's southern side,
Only acknowledging his sovereignty,
When, distant, unexercised its rule might be ;
And yet, on every side, surrounded, he
Perceived himself, while mad, ungoverned rage
Still prompted him, the futile war to wage,
—Miscalculating effort—to engage
In further outrage now against the king :
In this continued feud and suffering,
Each member of his family, defeat
Disastrously incurred and woe complete.

CII.

But yet, he was not warned ; and when he knew,
The ravaging, wild Saxons, on the North,
Imperatively called the monarch forth,
Who, late confiding in his promise true,

Left but the garrison armed with a few:
Lupo, from his mountain fastness, saw
How slow the heavy horses, forced to draw
The baggage and the treasure, up the steep
And shelving footholds—o'er the torrents deep
Of rocky buttressed hills, involving woods
All trackless—and defiles, and mountain floods;
Or, if a road—the skirting hillside's base
Above the rugged precipice, its place—
Where ambush and concealment might beset,
The way, on every side—a wary net.

CIII.

Then Lupo's purpose did in thought awake;
How easy it would be to undertake,
The prompt destruction of the king's rear guard,
With probable success—rapine's reward
Was sure, he knew, and punishment remote:
As flame-like, ghastly lights, o'er marshes float,
His wild thoughts quickly flashed, and then grew
    faint;
The consequence—the king's wrath he might paint
In vivid colors to his wavering mind;
—But who hath reckless will, that is not blind—
And then the chance, and the revenge so near,
Were cherished most, and—dominant o'er fear.

CIV.

The king was suffered, undisturbed, to pass
With the first great division of his host—
The weight of baggage made the second mass
    *14

Linger behind; and its commander's post
Was Roland's—dangerous, as he might dare:
—Anselm and Eggiard, cousins, did share
His watchful duty and unceasing care—
All doomed to suffer, most from unforeseen
Disaster terrible—where darkly lean,
Even to-day, the deep and dense high wood
Where long, and vainly strong, Roland withstood
The onslaught of the Gascons:—sudden life
Seemed bristling all the hillsides, and the strife
Of distant arrows, quickly sped, that fell:
—The Franks were forced down to the bottom dell
Of Roncevalles; and still the Gascons pressed
Triumph insatiate, that death confessed.

CV.

There the brave Franks, in iron-armor, driven,
Embarrassed by their arms, confused, and riven
From the main body, fought with desperate zeal—
But nothing could their ambushed fate repeal;
And, knowing not the road-ways, they were blind
With blood, and with their doubts, comrades to find
From foes inveterate:—thus Roland's friend,
Truest and dearest, Oliver the brave,
Did, in such sudden madness, o'er him bend—
Who gladly offered life, his friend's to save,
A thousand times, as they fought, side by side,
With valor equal, and with equal pride;
Now, blind with his own blood, he felled a blow,
On the bright brow—'twas Roland he struck low,
Who, reeling faint, rebounded quick again,

His sterner ardor now enchafed with pain :
—The nearest knights clung round him, and the fold
Of his rich standard staunched the wound that bled;
One glance he gave its broidered arms of gold;
Then, like a stag at bay, he shook his head,
And once more to the centre, forward sped,
O'er many a Gascon pillowed on his shield,
And many a brave companion of the field,
That in the equal conflict would not yield.

CVI.

Maddened, he saw not, if the glittering hoof
Struck on the cuirass of some pulseless heart,
With sparkling, ruthless speed—where death was
    proof,
No pang of crushing steel could make them start—
Swift bounding o'er them—his dread pathway lay:
Hopeless, he knew the desperate, fatal day,
And sought his last stand in the thickest fray:
—In the dense ambush of the deepest glade,
Close ranged the spikes of iron palisade;
And yet, the narrow stream its pathway made
Down through the center of the long defile,
Whose steep declivity reached o'er a mile:
Bold each sharp pinnacle—sublime and bluff,
Oppressed with grandeur—we behold enough :
A fortressed castle on the southern end,
Its narrow, deep-set windows, gleaming, send
Slant light into the darkness, weaving shapes—
Their hollow, muffled veils strange beauty drapes
Around the wild flowers and the mountain ash,
And where the torrents o'er their barriers dash.

CVII.

All the high woods still bristled into life—
They came—the Gascons to the bloody strife:
Many, entangled in the fray, once calling
Defiance or farewell to friend or foe,
Swooned to the bottoms, where the wrenched rock
    falling,
Drowned their last struggles in the surge below—
The stream was red with battle—dark with death,
And soundful with the pangs of parting breath—
A disentangled rest for foe and foe:
—Then here, at last, Lupo and Roland met,
The tide of battle not determined yet:
Lupo had stormed the fortress, and had won
The outer gates—resistance nearly o'er:
" Sons of Abu Taurus ! one blow more,
And the proud effort of achievement's done ! "
But at this moment rose a mighty shout
That changed the fierce, long struggle into rout :
" Turn to the utmost, craven ! *a l'outrance!*
Turn to the closest point thy gleaming lance !
Here are my fellows—only thirty left—
That through thy net of ambush. pathways cleft! "

CVIII.

As meteors burn that burst in midnight skies,
Lupo, on Roland, turned his blazing eyes
In wrath's defiance and in half surprise—
Giving no response, asking no retreat ;
Knowing at once that death must share defeat,
He felled his cimeter, flashing and fleet:

—Swift as the lightning that in storm-clouds play,
His lance, a hundred glittering fragments lay;
Roland's last vengeance *might* retaliate--
But no, he played with chance, reserving fate;
Partly, because he wished revenge to sate
Its last, deep justice on his dastard foe,
And that he might, himself, some final blow
Receive—for, all the anguish of his soul
At sight of Lupo, stirred its deep control.

CIX.

He parried quickly, and still held the strife,
A moment, sometimes at the point of life,
Till Lupo's horse with one loud, anguished neigh,
Falling in struggle, on his rider lay:
Roland dismounted on the bloody soil,
And helped his enemy to rise—" No foil
Or accident shall bar our mutual hate!
We stand together, now defend your fate!
There, still your sword, and here still flashes mine,
Our lives the vantage, and strong death the line
Of stern, divided strife! the Red-Cross sign
And thy pale Crescent well are matched, Lupo,
And in one grave, to-night, must slumber low!"
Again their swords crossed, but the sanguine flow
Of Roland's wounded brow warned him, that faint
Cessation must come o'er him soon: no plaint
Stirred his proud lip, till staggering—he paled:
Lupo perceived this chance, and quick availed
His lifted cimeter to end the strife ;—

One keen, relentless thrust—but Roland, rife
With latent energy in death's last throe,
Gave him, in turn, an unexpected blow :
—The Gascons were the victors in that fight ;

But Lupo never knew his triumph's might—
Dead, beside Roland—there they lay—those two :
Above them, that same night, falling the dew
Alike on each; the enmity, they knew,
Beneath it—coldly quenched—the false—the true.

CX.

Was it at sunset or at dawn of day
This battle terrible—no records say;
So great was the defeat. so dear the slain,
That history withheld, much of the pain
Of its recital while lived Charlemagne;
And, after the great life of that great king,
So much romance and record to it cling,
That we are left in wonder—wondering.
—Roland threw off his helmet, ere his fall ;
And where it dropped, the grass took crimson stain;
And ever since, a flower's coronal,
In sweet remembrance of it, doth remain,
Blooming in that deep dell of Pyrenees,
And called for it, in tryst of his last peace,
The " Casque de Roland," bright in sun and breeze;
And on the mountain there is shown a rock;
Hollowed, indented by the riving shock,
When there he struck his great sword "Durandal"
To shatter it—what hand could e'er recall
The valor that had wielded it ?—alone

It perished in *his* hand—cold as a stone—
The fiery flint *that* magic steel must own:
And this is why that rocky cleft, to-day—
A curving line across the mountain's way,
Is shown—the " Breche de Roland," so they say.

CXI.

And at his horn's last, marvelous, sweet sound,
The forest birds fell dead for miles around ;
Its long, clear peal of agony intense
Startled the king, and thrilled his fear's quick sense,
Who heard it at *St. Jean :* " I must go hence,"
He said, " that sound is Roland's dying blast,
And his defeat and death it doth forecast ! "
—And so it was :—there, shivered, near the stream,
His bright blade long invincible—bereft
Of all its valiant ardor ; and the gleam,
Through the dark sedges of the strong shield, cleft,
—Its gilded arabesque, from crown to base,
Once the fond care of armor-bearers—now
Lending its lustre to the pallid face,
And lying heavily upon the brow,
That, it had shielded oft—o'er that wild spot,
The eve closed ; and the combat he forgot.

CXII.

We see him in the red dust, where he fell;
We know how throbbed the high heart's parting
    swell ;
How tight the broken hilt in his closed hand,
How firm the closed lip from its last command:

Among the slain, the fairest and the best,
Close to the sanguine sward, his pale cheek pressed:
—How soft the starlight and the moonlight rose
After the tumult, o'er the dread repose !
No sob, no sound upon the evening's close;
Love, that had mourned him, was where weeping's
    stilled:
Night deepened, and soft winds through pine
    boughs thrilled:
Wrapt in his own cooled blood—a crimson pall—
Amidst the woods and hills of Roncevalles—
Dear—dead—and beautiful ! and that is all !

CXIII.

The Convent of Nonnenwerth still is seen
From Roderberg's height where the turrets lean:
And nature, who deviates not her way,
Is still as she was in the olden day :
Still the rays of morn, over Rolandseck,
On the Lake of Nonnenwerth, softly break;
And the Convent windows reflect the light
From the basalt pinnacle, steep and bright;
And green is the Isle, in the Island stream,
As a radiant emerald in its gleam :
Still the Vesper bells of the Convent ring,
And the fringing willows their shadows fling—
Dusk-waving willows, full of trembling gloom,
Where strangers linger near her quiet tomb;
And there she sleepeth, for a thousand years—
Her sweet eyes closed upon the troubled tears:
Surely, God gave, at last, the just reward

" Still the Vesper bells of the Convent ring,
    And the fringing willows their shadows fling—
    Dusk-waving willows, full of trembling gloom,
    Where strangers linger near her quiet tomb;
    And there she sleepeth, for a thousand years—
    Her sweet eyes closed upon the troubled tears."

Page 216.—Stanza CXIII.

Of her blessing lost, unto Hildegarde!
Let us hope, her joy had in Heaven birth,
Beyond the sorrow she had known on Earth!

CXIV.

She looks, no more, up to the tower height;
She looks, no more, upon love's flower blight—
Where the Arch moulders, and the peristyles,
In the last radiance of the sunset-smiles!
—In despair's surcease Roland built that tow'r
Of love's watch lingering, hour after hour,
When his faithful heart lived and wept, alone,
In bitter anguish that is dead and gone!
—Fair is " Rascida Vallis "— far and fair—
The " Casque de Roland " is still blooming there!
Should you walk beside its bright, crimson bell,
Sit down and list to what the maidens tell,
For I have told it, not one-half, so well!
There's the " Breche de Roland "—its fissure deep;
And chapel where he lieth, long asleep!
And may its memories thy kind heart keep;
For true this story, though the fate so hard,
Of faithful Roland and fair Hildegarde!

NOTES.

Note 1.—Stanza V.

Blown seaward unto thee, O Golden Gate;

"Blows with a perfume of songs and memories,
Blows from the capes of the past over sea to the bays of the
present."—*Swinburne's Hesperia.*

Note 2.—Stanza VII.

The night had come! Mons. Jovis under snow,

Mons. Jovis was the ancient name of Mount St. Bernard. A
temple of Jupiter formerly occupied the site of the present famous
monastery.

Note 3.—Stanza X.

Byzantine fabrics from the cities old:

There was a sort of cloth known to the ancients, and called
Bysus, the quality of its texture is not now exactly known,—
whether cotton, linen, or silk—is a matter of dispute.

Note 4.—Stanza XI.

An Indian Goddess of Tanjore's great shrine;

The magnificence of the East Indian temples is well known to
the reader, particularly those of the Deccan, and the more southern
portion of India: Their structure is peculiar; in many instances
they are excavated out of the rocky hillsides, as are those of Ele-
phanta, and Kenneri, and the great cave of Carli;—spacious, lofty
and richly sculptured. The pyramidal temples called Pagodas, are
also numerous in the south of India; but in grandeur and beauty,
they are all eclipsed by that of *Tanjore*,—a city long celebrated as
the most learned and opulent in the south of India. Previous
to 1833 Lord Valentia gave a cursory account of its wonderful temple, although he was not allowed to enter its sacred precincts, but
from the door he obtained a view of the interior, which contained
the gigantic figure of a bull, in black granite; this revered animal
was a favorable specimen of Hindoo sculpture.

NOTE 5.—STANZA XVII.

Surprised Noureddin in his mighty tent,

Gilbert De Lacy, Knight Templar, was one of the Crusaders possessing English fiefs: He accomplished this dangerous feat in the reign of Stephen; I have inserted it, although occurring a century or two later than the theme of the poem—with that desire of adding to romance, historic incident, and with perhaps a little of the pardonable pride, of a great precedent,—Sir Walter Scott, who introduced his ancestral name of Scott, in his "Lay of the last Minstrel."

NOTE 6.—STANZA XVIII.

Like webs in winter, rock to rock enlaced;

The banks of the Arno on either side, are flanked by plantations of the olive and vine, the deep blue green of the former contrasting strikingly with the light verdure of the vine leaves. They are planted in alternate rows; and the intervening soil frequently made to yield a crop of barley. Towards evening we saw a few fireflies, but these beautiful and remarkable insects do not appear to flourish in Europe as in the East, where they convert the whole atmosphere into a galaxy of twinkling stars. The cicada made a prodigious chirping by the road side; almost the whole way from Rome it kept up an incessant noise, scarcely audible when the carriage was in motion, but sufficient to stun the ear the moment of a halt.—*Notes of a Wanderer—W. F. Cumming, M. D.*

NOTE 7.—STANZA XIX.

These were the haunting Gnomes of Whisperthal;

The Whisper is a small tributary of the river Rhine, regarded by the inhabitants with awe, on account of its voiceful cadences. The Stone of Lorch is not far from it, on which the Gnomes are supposed to sacrifice young ladies unless they are rescued.

NOTE 8.—STANZA XXI.

Whose roofless walls amid the forest stand—

The ruins of Ehrenfels are lonely and beautiful, in the forest of Niederwald. The Chapel of St. Roch is above it on the hill, and the views in the neighborhood are in keeping with the sublimity of the Beech and Oak shades of Niederwald. The luxuriant vineyards of Rudesheim are in the vicinity.

NOTE 9.—STANZA XXVII.

But who were Hunald and the feared Lupo?

Eudes, the father of Hunald, had leagued with the Saracens, against Charles Martel, who still triumphed, and forgave his apostacy, and his enmity. After the death of Eudes his territories were

divided between his three sons, and his repugnance to the French
was transmitted with his territories; Hunald, who was the oldest
of the sons, received Aquitaine for his portion, but was soon
forced to submit to Charles, though the spirit of revolt still existed.
Hatton was blinded by his brother, Hunald, in order that he
might acquire supremacy; but disappointment and remorse—the
continued defeat of his efforts at revolt, made the courage of Hunald sink, and in disgust he gave a temporary farewell to the world,
resigning his Dukedom to his son Waifer, he retired into a Monastery. Waifer was equally turbulent and so it went, Hunald subsequently leaving the Monastery, and again calling all Aquitaine to
arms. Lupo was the cousin of Waifer, and the nephew of Hunald; whether Abu Taurus was the other brother of Hunald is a
question, but Lupo was really the nephew of Hunald. The early
accounts of those personages vary, according to different authorities:
I have, perhaps, taken advantage of this as far as some slight
changes of time, place or character, allowable to historic romance,
in some of the statements. Abu Taurus was really a Saracen emir,
and whether Lupo's family had intermarried with the Mohammedans is not on record, but merely supposition, on the grounds that
such marriages had become occasional, especially between the
Christians of the Asturias, and the Saracens, the latter having gained supremacy over them. There is recently published a new edition
of the original Eginhard's life of Charlemagne, but I have refer-
ence to the version of G. P. R. James, whose notes from Eginhard are very extensive, together with notes from the annals called
Loisclani, and others. This is also true as to the remarks in the
preface of Nonnenwerth about Roland's parentage and place of
burial.

NOTE 10.—STANZA XXX.

In shady dells the Maccabees had passed,

The ruins of this castle are on the road from Gaza to Jerusalem,
and the more modern village of Kobab is not far from it. Near by,
are the remains of an ancient Christian church, the castle and
church are mentioned by Curson, and must have been still in good
preservation, during the eighth century.

NOTE 11.—STANZA XXXI.

The Pools of Gihon where a King was crowned,

Solomon.

NOTE 12.—STANZA XXXIII.

There were some pious merchants selling beads,

Although the Rosary in its present form, was not used so early
as the date mentioned, yet, a sort of chaplet for numbering

prayers was in existence.—Pebbles and other things were used for the same purpose. The Mohammedans use a Rosary something like that of the Christians.

Note 13.—Stanza XXXV.

The Holy Cross, long hidden from all view.

The Holy Cross, and the crosses of the two thieves, after the crucifixion were thrown into the town ditch, or as some accounts state, into an old vault near by; here they were soon covered by the refuse of the city. The Empress Helena made a pilgrimage to Jerusalem, in her old age, and threatened all the Jewish inhabitants with torture and death, if they did not produce the Holy Cross from the place where their ancestors had concealed it,—one old fellow who was said to possess authentic information, was nearly starved, in prison, when he consented to reveal the secret. The Legends of the Cross are numerous and some of them poetically beautiful. The old Jew mentioned, petitioned heaven, whereupon the earth trembled, soon a sweet odor issued forth—the soil in that spot being removed, the three crosses were discovered, together, with the superscription belonging to the principal one, whose identity then became a fresh anxiety to the Empress,—giving rise to those numerous speculations that are since extant, and so full of mystic analogy.

Note 14.—Stanza XXXVIII.

Such was really the impressive and princely gift of Haroun Al Raschid to Charlemagne—the keys of the Holy City and the Christian standard.

Note 15.—Stanza L.

I am exacting as the King Clovis,

The name of Clovis is remembered as much on account of the vase of Soissons, as for any event of his reign. It is thought, this elegant vase belonged to the Sacred buildings of Rheims which were despoiled of many articles of value. It was of immense size and exceedingly curious workmanship. St. Remi, the eloquent and talented Bishop of Rheims, whose fame at this time was spreading through Gall, had influence with Clovis, and asked him to restore the vase. "Follow me to Soissons," replied the King to the messengers, "there the booty is to be divided, and if it be in my power, the prelate's desire shall be gratified." On their arrival at Soissons the troops assembled, and the mass of the plunder lay in a glittering heap, waiting to be portioned off, each man according to his lot. The King turning to the soldiers whom he had so often led to victory—pointed to the magnificent vase and desired that it might be assigned to him; many of the soldiers at once consented, but one, jealous of the invasion of the usual custom, or

hoping to obtain the prize himself, raised his axe and dashed it
down on the vase, exclaiming in answer to the King's demand,
"thou shalt have nothing here but that which fortune shall give
thee by lot." For a moment all was silent consternation, but the
general voice assigning the vase to Clovis, it was returned,
although so sadly injured, to the messenger of the Bishop. It may
be supposed a barbarian monarch would find it not easy to suppress
his resentment at so great an outrage and provocation, and his
power and popularity were sufficient to uphold him in any meas-
ure, however extreme against the culprit, but with strong self control, he maintained that composure to which he owed his supremacy, and power over his subjects. One year after, at the general
assembly of the people, in the Champs de Mars, when according to
the custom, all the warriors presented themselves before the monarch to show that their arms and equipments were kept in good
order, the young soldier who had broken the vase presented himself with signs of negligence in the condition of his weapons, in
any event, such accusation could easily be made for slight cause,
and when he stood before the King, the latter exclaimed in wrath,
"None show themselves here with such arms as thine,—thy lance,
thy battle axe, all, are disgraceful to a soldier!" The young man
stooped in silence to pick up his axe from where the King had
thrown it, but as he did so, Clovis with a blow of his weapon
called a *francisque*, smote him to the ground never to rise again,
saying, "so did'st thou strike the vase of Soissons."

NOTE 16.—STANZA LI.

Each shoulder marked, each shell-medallioned hat,

A scallop-shell on the front of the broad brimmed hat, and the
red cross embroidered or braided on the left shoulder of the cloak
destinguished the returned pilgrim.

NOTE 17.—STANZA LII.

The Duke Friuli, and brave Count Gerold,

Heric, Duke of Friuli, commanded an immense and willing
army against the Huns, for Charlemagne, and returned with the
largest booty that had ever been captured by any of his armaments,
a portion of this was taken to Rome by Angelbert. Count Gerold
was another of Charlemagne's officers, who with the Duke of
Friuli commanded the forces on the frontier of Saxony; he was
slain while addressing his army preparatory to a general battle.
The Duke Friuli was also subsequently led into ambush and killed
with all, his followers.

NOTE 18.—STANZA LXII.

Loud voices called Campulus and Paschal,

The hatred which Campulus and Paschal, the two disappointed
aspirants to the Papacy had conceived against the more successful

Leo, had slumbered, but was not extinct. The ecclesiastical sit-
uations held by the two factions of Romans and the favor with
which they were regarded by the unsuspecting Leo himself, gave
them many opportunities of revenge. They hoped by a mixture of
boldness and art to escape the consequence of their crime. The
moment they chose for the perpetration of their design was while
the Pope, attended by all the clergy and followed by the
populace, rode through a part of the city performing what they
called the Greater Litany. Paschal and Campulus were placed
close to the person of the Chief Pontiff, and are said to have received from him some new mark of kindness on that very morning.
All passed tranquilly till the line of the procession approached the
monastery of St. Stephen and St. Sylvester, and even then, the banners and crosses, the clerks and chorists which preceeded were
permitted to advance till suddenly as the higher clergy began to
traverse the space before the building, armed men were seen mingling among the people. The march of the procession was ob-
structed. A panic seized both the populace and the clergy, all fled
but Campulus, Paschal and their abettors, and Leo was left
alone in the hands of the conspirators. The Pontiff was immediately assailed and cast upon the ground, and with eager and trembling hands—for crime is generally fearful—the traitors proceeded
to attempt the extinction of his sight and the mutilation of his
tongue. It is possible that the struggles of their unfortunate victim
disappointed the strokes of the conspirators, and that his exhaustion
from terror, exertion and loss of blood deceived them into the
belief that they had more than accomplished their purpose;
dispersing the moment the deed was committed, the chief conspirators left the apparently lifeless body of the prelate to be dragged
into the monastery of St. Erasmus.—*See Life of Charlemagne by G.
P. R. James, Esq.*

WHERE SHE SLEEPS IN SANTA CLARA. *

———

SO stately and pale, my Lady, you sleep,
    First falling leaves of the winter wind sweep
Down on thy fair feet, and over thy head;
Thy sensitive lips have not a word said,
Of the cold or the rain for many a week:
Can it be I still would list them to speak,
And they do not ?—from thy bonny brown eye
A glance never more,—I lean tenderly,
Where I only may see, oval and dark,
Thy bed hollowed out in the wild-wood park,
Where the bird shall linger, that comes in spring,
A sad sweet singer who will lift his wing
And leave more lonely the spot of thy rest,
As trembles his shadow across thy breast :
There are walks where thy feet no more may tread,
Like the mid-summer rose, thy bloom is fled:
We kissed thee, and covered, and called thee dead.

---

* The author's mother, who died October 18th, 1879.

*15

But to thy freed spirit, are other things   .
Than the birds that droop with o'er-wearied wings,
Or the autumn sun's dim, declining rays,
O'er thy burial-place after vanished days,—
Not so vainly sweet as the cross and wreath,
We left there to perish the first lone eve ;
Serenely secure now *thy* hope and faith,
While, alas ! forever *we* love and grieve !

CHRISTMAS EVE, 1879.

"ET ELLE EST MUETTE."

POWERS' GREEK SLAVE.

THERE is no quiver in the grace that lies
    Across her downcast eyes:
And out of marble hath a chisel made,
The quiet, pallid hands so languid laid—
Naked, and with your eyes upon her set,
"Et elle est muette."

The fine round wrist where hang the modeled links,
Stirs not, throbs not, nor shrinks ;
No glow of glorious rose burns in her cheek—
Donato's could not, neither can *she*, speak ;
Is she thy love ? O sculptor desolate !
"Et elle est muette."

"Marco, par che non mi parli ? " *   Ah, no!
That Mark did never answer Angelo !
O Powers! fame is thine o'er all the earth :
But from her lips no sound of grief or mirth,
Thy spell of silence there, unbroken yet
"Et elle est muette."

REMEMBRANCE.

NOW, the blue light of manly eyes
    Stirs in my heart no grieved surprise,
If passion's veiled in their sweet grace,
    I only see thine absent face.
The footstep that could hush my heart
To hear, is thine ; so far apart.
    I know, I say, so like to him,
    And with sweet tears my eyes are dim ;
The hurt of human feeling, worn
As though thy rose had dropped a thorn !

---

* One of the bronze statues of Donato de Bardi, a St. Mark,
was so admirably executed that, on first seeing it, Michael Angelo
addressed it in these emphatic words: "Marco, par che non mi
parli ?" Mark, why do you not speak to me ?

AN ANSWER.

INSCRIBED TO MRS. R. R———N.

The pearl and purple of thy gentle eyes,
So wistful, asking me for song or sign:
What thoughts, my friend, my dear, shall I entwine
For thy demanding heart?   What true replies?

Shall I say that thine eyelids drooped, and strove
With the blind, bitter tears that fell between?
Wherefore, I need not tell thee what hath been,
So well thou knowest, Lady of my love!

Or might I tell of the sweet interspace,
Wherein thy bright lips sighed and grew more pale,
Though wearing smiles, not less sweet, for a veil—
But through all still beholding—What rare face!

The curled waves of the gold sea in the sun,
Are the same garments of the shoreward tide:
He, too, gained Paradise, who had denied;
Belief and disavowal—are they one?

Sorrow and joy, my dear—are they two things?
The coral-footed dove that doth alight,
Is she not just the same that taketh flight,
Afar, afar, on her white lifted wings?

LAMENT OF

LEONORA D'ESTE.

AN ANSWER TO THE "LAMENT OF TASSO."

It is now generally considered, that the suffering and imprisonment of Tasso, at the hands of Alphonzo of Este, the brother of Leonora, were owing to the unhappy love of Tasso for Leonora; there is much speculation existing on the parts of *J. H. Wiffen*, *Foscolo*, and some refutation on the part of *Serassi* as to the regard of Leonora for Tasso;—and Byron seems to accept the conclusion that Leonora loved Tasso, while she dared not give much testimony of this regard. It may be supposed that a princess of the house of Este would not seem to encourage the poor poet, but the latter in a conzone to her, appealingly said: "Chi mi guido?" "What star guided me hither and promised me hope?" All the presumptions of probability and all the arguments of reason concur to answer Leonora. Such are the opinions of Wiffen and Foscolo, whom he quotes. Byron, also, who turned when at Farrara with more interest to the prison cell of Tasso in the hospital of St. Anna than he did to the monument of Aristo, seems to be convinced of Leonora's responsive love; even while he makes Tasso doprecate her reserve in the famous "Lament" he expresses the existence of some *secret hope* as witness the following:

> "I told it not, I breathed it not; it was
> Sufficient to itself—its own reward,
> And if my eyes reveal'd it, they, alas !
> Were punished by the silentness of thine;
> *And yet I did not venture to repine.*"

The italics are introduced in the present quoting to show Byron's accredited opinion that Tasso was convinced in his *secret hopes*, whatever may have been the expression of his discontent at the adversity of circumstances. And again he makes Tasso say: "And thou, Leonora; thou who wert ashamed that such as I could love, —*who blushed to hear—*." Byron, in his researches of old Italian manuscripts and libraries had perhaps a better chance than either Wiffen or Foscolo of forming an opinion on this subject. In the above lines he expresses that *peculiar fear* which accompanies the responsive love of a woman so placed as Leonara, without which there would be *indifference* and not *love*, and in the presence of which there is love, *trembling and true*. Again, a few lines' lower down, so sure does Tasso seem of Leonora's suffering in common with his own that he incites Leonora to go and reproach her brother with their *mutual misery*—

> "Go tell thy brother that my heart untamed
> By grief, years of weariness, and it may be
> A taint of that he would impute to me,
> From long infection of a den like this
> Where the mind rots congenial with the abyss,
> Adores thee still:—and add—that when the towers,
> And battlements which guard his joyous hours,
> Of banquet, dance, and revel, are forgot,
> Or left untended in a dull repose,
> This—this, shall be a consecrated spot.
> *But thou—when all that birth and beauty throws*
> *Of magic round thee is extinct,—shalt have*
> *One half the laurel that o'ershades my grave.*"

This prophecy is now incontrovertible, not less from the pen of Byron than from the sorrowful forethought of Tasso, and since so many have tendered sympathetic tribute to Tasso in this:—the following lines are in the same spirit inscribed by their author to the memory of Leonora of Este :

————

Bᴇ thou at rest, where silence folds her wing,
    My dove, in "clefts of rock," by strange seas
broken ! *
I speak or smile, I dream awhile or sing ;
    And yet to thee, send never word or token !

————

* "My dove in the clefts of the rock, in the hollow places of the wall, show me thy face."—*Solomon's Canticles.*

Say, love, they're censer fires with lid unraised·
    Or Druid wands with mystic leaf and meaning!
He was not spoken *to*, whom angels praised—
    His throne is veiled, whereon are seraphs leaning !

* * * * ✿

But I will know thee, in the dreamy close
    Of music, and the drench of water-flowers—
In the high dome's imperial repose,
    When day is turning into twilight hours !
        And, oh, when sobs break on some midnight
        sleep,
    Sweet love its tryst shall keep !

What though, with pealing glory of renown,
    My dark bereavement yet should crownéd be,
Still would I gaze far up to where thy throne
    Is out of reach, O brow, that beams on me !
        Some earthward angel's pinion, widely spread,
        Its glory, on thee shed !

O gentle brow of rarely templed thought,
    Avails it now to breathe o'er thee this pain ?
Hath thy soul, casements whose deep stillness caught
    The radiance of strange hours that pale and wane,
        Till one might deem their marble chaplets, not
        The flowers a sculptor wrought ?

✿ ✿ ✿ ✿ ✿

Speak, I would say to thee, but that I fear
    I could not bear this weight of yearning ; then

Too dear thou should'st become, too doubly dear—
   And *such* a prince of woe, my Lord of men !
How could I bear it, so ?—this life apart,
   With but the voiceful linger of thy breath
On some chance hour—thine eyes fire all my heart,
   Till day is misery and night is death !

Alas ! that I might say, wake not this pain !
   My slumbrous soul is half contented now!
Think ! the world's sentence would but call it "stain,"
   My kiss, too happy on thy lover brow !
And yet, pride—falling from its stronger morn,
   Over that altar of fair majesty—
Would dare, in clustered roses, any thorn
   To pierce the wayward feet that strayed to thee !

I do believe thee, love, so kingly wise,
   Turned on me fondly, almost deified !
I do believe thee—raised are drooping eyes
   To question if, for this, was love denied—
To question if, for this, was love long tried ?
   That herein I may find it, changed, transposed,
Life's marvel doubted, till the wounded side,
   All of its mystery and truth, disclosed !

Deity, doubt, pain, life—all stand confessed—
   Sorrow, so silent for its just reproof—
Faith's late, sad surety that had been blessed,
   Had it believed—not trusting, stood aloof!
Speak to me, love !   Though silent, I adore thee !
   E'en when I do not lift mine eyes to meet

Thy looks, so veiled!   O sacred shrine before me,
 Silence is peace—yet, were assurance sweet!

Speak to me, then, when near me, at some fall
 Of night, upon the lonely, lonely sea!
When thy dear presence is so near that all
 Its majesty of stillness shadeth me!
Till I could kneel, in my excess of feeling
 And voiceless happiness, close to thy side,
For the dumb answer of the bliss, revealing
 How I had hoped, and had not been denied!

   ✿ ✿ ✿ ✿ ✿

Oh, *I* would speak to *thee!* Oh that I might!
 Love, wilt thou hear me, in this voiceless pain?
I am alone, and the still pall of night
 Is over all things—the deep, low refrain
Of spirit music, on the wandering wind,
 Haunts earth's broken places, like the thoughts of
  thee,
Seeking for rest within my heart—to find,
 Only the billows of a troubled sea!
Ah, dost thou make this sweet and heavy thought—
 My heart already weary—this deep sigh,
That finds its echo mid the things unsought,
 Because of their deep dread? Ah! mournfully,
'Twill hover round thee ever,* music made
 To thy soul's symphony!   The unseen throne

---

  * No power in death can tear our names apart,
  As none in life could rend thee from my heart.
  Yes, Leonora, it shall be our fate
  To be entwined forever—but too late.
     —*Byron's Lament of Tasso.*

Of heaven, its bright splendors burn and fade
  In lonely human hearts, with none to own !
Oh, that thou wert near me! that I might weep
  Upon thy bosom and be not afraid !
Oh, then, methinks, that I could calmly sleep,
  And yet, the very thought's with dread arrayed !
Although there is no peace but in the deep
  Of thy gentle eyes,—there, fond fancies lead,
And I am quiet, until time unbroken
  Wreathes me a garland till the moments speed
To where falls the real, and the fair token
  Is borne away, where I may see it never,
With the lost life-beats of the heart's wild fever !

Oh, this is over me, as mystic sleep
  That is not earthly sleep, nor earthly waking,
Where voices whisper soft, and dark eyes weep,
  And lips grow pearly o'er the heart's deep breaking !
Though I have said forget me, it is well—
  Though thou hast said forget me, as its knell,
That we should never meet, and never part—
  To risk that anguish, where a tide may swell
Its surge of waves, to each o'er beating heart !
  Full of thy deep, deep love—the waters wail ;
And so I fear not, though it mournful be,
  For in the mist that shrouds thee, like a vail,
I see my Lord's hand raised o'er Galilee ;
  "And then I know," He said, "that this should be !"
But when thy voice told me I should forget,
  And thy dear hand had silenced hope's sweet key,
I hushed the thrill that murmured with regret,

And made my soul obey thee, silently!
But oft it waked with haunting voices fraught,
   That whispered e'er of thee *Forget me not!*

Thou wert not doomed to ever be forgot—
   Yet, didst thou say to me a low good-bye,
With trembling words whose meaning was unsought
   Of the sweet spirit in thy heart and eye!
And thou didst leave me with a last look taken,
   Like that, the soul doth take in changing dreams
Vainly to realize I was forsaken—
   And yet, I was remembered as the streams
That trill their mournful music on the ear,
   All listless, lying where the woodland teems
With unblessed words of mysteries as fair
   As the soul of the dreamer lying there!
But I was happy—heavy though it were
   To dwell on earth, of thy dear love unblessed—
For haunting melodies gave promise rare,
   And light in thy dear eyes, I ne'er had guessed,
When all earth's shadows shall in quiet rest,
   Morning and night, upon each pulseless breast!

I dreamed of thee, methought a temple fair
   Was o'er us, and its lighted aisles were teeming,
And pale and sad thou wert, lone standing there,
   In a dense throng, but to my fond eyes, seeming,
Noble in proud grace, as I know thou art!
   How trembled my glad heart even in dreaming,
As a rose-cloud at eve, that zephyrs part!
   Thou didst not see me, in the crowded maze

Where stood so many whom I did not know ;
   Soon fire swept round us, and the fearful blaze
Undermined the frail timbers neath our feet :
   Then seeing all my danger—the great woe
That swept thy fair brow, to my heart, was sweet !
   No word thy pale lip passed—a silent look
Gave me alone the meaning of its sorrow,
   But though the hope of life my heart forsook—
Knowing that night of fire would have no morrow,
   Born of that hopelessness—thy faithful love,
That look of thine—a life might never prove !
   I did not perish, and I tried to win thee,
And rocked my feet upon the swaying pile ;
   But many glided in the throng between thee
And where lone I stood, gazing down the aisle
   My eyes still saw thy sweet, pale lips compressed,
I wakened, yearning for thy silent breast !

Why did I look upon thy radiant brow ?
   Though so blest my eyes, gazing on its light ;
But weeping bitterly, my heart's voice low
   Then claimed from me some lost, forgotten right !
I dare not think or feel what this may be,
   Life's hope and death's indifference lie there,
A lonely wreck upon a drifting sea—
   To look on its abyss, I do not dare :
Oh, let me strive while linger hope and prayer ?
   I could not see my God ! for oh, I fear,
There is a cave rock-bound, which he forgot,
   Where the mad surges lash the rocks so drear.
That chaos dirges ever—"He is not !"

Oh, I dare not listen—I turn away!
No rest, no rest! for hand, or foot, or heart!
    Turmoil and strife must ever be their sway!
I ask, ye winds, which gains the victor's part?
    Eternal life, or Lethe's unseen deep?
Ye moan and mourn, but still ye answer not—
    Still unrevealed, that pale and mystic sleep!
Shall the heart's beatings be all then forgot?
    Oh, no! I cannot give them up!—their love
Is all too torturing—too thrilling sweet!
    Their living restless throes immortal prove
The soul that makes the heart thus wildly beat!

Oh, I remember when my proud heart reigned,
    Like an immortal dove, within my breast,
But struggling long, her heavy wing hath strained,
    Since o'er the waves, long sought—no place of rest!
A passionate appeal I make to thee—
    Should that deep moment come, when all soul-worn
Dark waters may come rushing over me!
    Oh, give me death with that sweet peace whose
        morn
Will rise in unknown splendor o'er the sea!
    Hide me in its waves, ere the night of scorn
Set ever round me by one look from thee!
    When my eyes close upon thy bosom's deep,
Kiss them, forever, to eternal sleep!

           ✿   ✿   ✿   ✿   ✿

For thy love's sake, Tasso, for thy love burning,
    And for the closed behests of waiting years,

Kept in the patience of a tried heart mourning,
   Under the arches of its quenchless tears !

Think of me, darling, when thy soul's deep hushes
   Grow wakeful in the light of some slow hour
Between the midnight and the opal gushes,
   When the dawn pleads with night and day for power!

Think of me, darling, in the clime divided
   From spring and summer, where glad tides ne'er
     come,
And, say, "Ah, me! sweet heart, from mine elided,
   I love thee yet, my love, though grief is dumb !

When thou art silent, for the sharp precision
   Of catching some deep memory gliding by,
Perhaps, dear love, such is my hour of vision,
   Thy spirit comes so near, and says, " 'Tis I ! "

Believe me, darling, when thy gladness, paling,
   Seems more than weary, like a mournful river,
The curse-born Eden of the unavailing
   Thinks of the gates again, where angels shiver !

Take them, the roses, on the lone heath blowing,
   And put them where thy breast is warm and white,
And when they die there, love, thou mayst be
     knowing
   They're but sweet allegories of a blight !

Thou'lt find the passion of thy lips which break
   Upon their leaves, and pulsing, beat apart
With thrills of thy soft breath, as when a lake
   Is stirred, as once you said, was stirred my heart !

Near where we stood, the dark, full summer-boughs
   Met over us in arches green and grand:
I was forgetful of the wasting glows
   That burued their life within thy cheek and hand !

Sweet censers, whence no earth may gather blame
   Or spirit meaning, any fire of dust—
The stone was rolled away, ere morning came,
   And watchers stood appalled before their trust !

What care that nothing shelters my lone head
   From falls of dew that damp each heavy tress,
Whose temples fail to coolness, that were fed
   To fever by thy glances' tenderness !

My *feet* were in the *dust* that should be sere,
   Over this head, ere heard those words of thine—
How near *thy heart* was, yet, "He had not where
   To lay his head"—*earth* and *heaven* his shrine !

What care, then, if the barren surge were spread
   Over me dirgeless, still, without thy voice
To break the turbid waste where tempests shed
   Their wrath's vain triumph o'er that one sweet
     choice !

Oh, mind me not ! though o'er my head no cover
   From winds and stars; tell me no more because
A soft warm hand, in seeming, falleth over
   A forehead claimless—a dear hand that was !

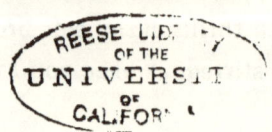

I dared its touch: *thy* hand, I reached for it,
  Fearing the glow, the pressures deep, strong thrill!
And yet, would God, it held me infinite,
  Through every pulsing tribute of Life's will !

In day-spring, dreams burn oft for thee, and ever,
  It seems, as thou art bending o'er me here !
Thy mouth's intense sweet sigh, its flush of fever—
  And, oh ! the arms, that draw me, near and near !

Alas ! wild dream, and heart of wild unrest—
  Loose life, I pray thee, from between thy throes—
My lover ! O my lover ! on thy breast,
  Pain, blame, and rapture could their bonds unclose!

Too well I know thee, vain, deep-kindling thought—
  In thy devotedness I'm doomed to be,
Like the coral fane Nereides wrought,
  A templed labor, and an agony !

Forget me then, forget that tortured wail,
  That mirage of regret, that rose afar—
For it the isle of founts hath no avail,
  Nor plumes of peace, nor light of vesper star !

Take them away ! O infinite sweet tone
  Keep thee, till soft grass bendeth in the spring,
Over me lowly, light, and windward blow—
  Then say, "Dear head, thou'rt crowned with
    everything !"

Oh, be not sad, if never more again
  By soft-winged verse or sign, thy love I move !
Too much to weep, and suffer—its refrain,
  To suffer and to weep—this were to love !

Too much of tears and strife would be its cost,
   Till heart on heart, their quest fall tremblingly,
To break, to beat, till heav'n and peace were lost—
   This cross is veiled, beloved ! So let it be !

* * * * *

Farewell, my dearest! hush thy loving heart,
   Whose silver lyre is beating that bright shore,
Beyond my heart's low sigh, where deep winds start,
   And bear the soft waves to the strand once more !

How can I bear it—all the dark, deep meaning
   That droops beside thy spirit ?   Had it been
In the white flush of young life's bright beginning,
   Ere blame had scorched it, or name called it sin !

Thy soul's sweet whisper through my being, sweeping,
   The anthem that on life is longest, deepest—
Oh, had it been before the time of weeping,
   Ere thou, this dumb regret, in vigil, keepest !

How had my heart not stopped to fear or ponder,
   How had it *then*, unbound, knelt at thine own,
Learning the colors in thine eyes' sweet wonder,
   And gath'ring life's deep joy from one sweet tone !

How had I loved thee, as thou shouldst be loved !
   How had I waited for each doubtful thrill—
That glance, or voice, or touch of thine had proved,
   Through all the glad life, at thy strong life's will !

*16

How had the troublous heart, o'erful with yearning,
  Been given, beat by beat, beneath thy breast—
A tide gone seaward, to its deep returning,
  The while thine eyes, like stars, beheld me blest !

But hush, O heart, before the thought thou darest,
  And count the links of chains and steps of time;
But do not count the heart-beats, which thou fearest,
  And do not call thy tenderest records crime !

STAR OF THE SEA.

—

In whom I am "well pleased"—the lone watch-towers
  Of Silence, and of Effort's sweet surcease—
Late hast thou lighted unto paths of Peace,
  Over the strong surf where long hung dark hours !

And now all brighter for severe contrast—
  Star of the Sea, to whom my looks have turned,
Footfalls of shepherds, as at first,—at last,
  Will stop, and know wherefore thy glory burned !

ALTSAY BURN.

In the early part of the seventeenth century, Angus, eldest son of the Glengarry Chief, Macdonnell, made a foray into the territory of the Clan Mackenzie in the frith of Beauly, with whom the Macdonnells were at war; on his way home from the fatal expedition the heir of Glengarry was intercepted and slain, with several of his followers, by a party of Mackenzies. To revenge his death, a strong body of Glengarry men were sent under Allen Mac Raonuill of Lundy, who led them immediately across the hills into the country of their enemies. Marching on Sunday morning, and finding a numerous company of the Mackenzies then at worship in the chapel of Cillie-Christ, near Beauly, they set fire to the church and burned the unsuspecting congregation, having previously secured every aperture of escape. Lips on which the orison was unfinished, now gave vent to the wildest shrieks of despair. Over the crackling, devouring flames and the shrieks of the victims, could be heard the shrill notes of the pibroch in malicious triumph, and the horrible sights and sounds were only darkened and silenced by the ashes of the funeral pile. When all was over the atrocious perpetrators retired from the scene, like troops after a victory, enjoying the dastardly satisfaction of having avenged their wrong. But the flames, by which the Mackenzies suffered, served as the gathering beacon to the clan; every man who could bear a sword now drew it forth and rushed to the pursuit, dividing their forces into two bodies, one following the track along the south side of Loch-Ness, while the other, crossing the mountains, on the north bank of the lake, pursued the first division of the Macdonnells under their leader, Mac Raonuill. Stimulated by revenge they continued the chase without intermission, and at length overtook the guilty fugitives near Altsay Burn, where they ventured to halt for rest. The hostile clans mutually fatigued, but still burning with hate, rushed on each other with deadly rancor, and for a time the conflict was desperately even, but at length the Macdonnells were driven into the *burn*, or torrent, where many of them missing the ford, and impeded by the rugged rocks of the channel, were overtaken and slain by the Mackenzies. Mac Raonuill, a man of athletic frame took a desperate leap and cleared the abyss, landing safely on the opposite bank. One of the Mackenzies swift in pursuit, leaped blindly, reckless of the danger, after him. The desperate venture of the daring pursuer failed; his feet falling short of the bank, he met with the tragic end as described. But the worsted party of the Macdonnells who had figured so remorselessly in the burning of the church that morning, were not, for all that, suffered to escape; they now fled by Inverness but were surprised in a public house by the other detachment of the Mackenzies, who made sure of their prey, surrounded the house, secured the doors and setting fire to the thatch, the flames burst forth in an instant. Thirty-seven of the Macdonnells did penance for their vicious proceedings of the morning. Such was the raid of Cillie-Christ, or Christ-Church, and the speedy retribution by which it was followed.—*See Beatie's Illustrated Scotland.*

I.

WHOSE side with flowery garlands hung,
 Whose winds with Ossian's harp had sung—
Whose dense, dark birch, the bottoms line,
With purple heath and feathery pine,
Made beautiful—whose gray rocks rise
In the repose of sunset skies:
—The azure, light-incumbent sky,
Reached unto, as by Alps as high,
Where straggling falls the knotty ash
From storm-reft ledges with a crash:
Where footsteps pause to seek return—
This is the gorge of Altsay burn,
Not all whose beauty here I tell,
But mark this much for what befell!

II.

Glengarry's chief held Angus dear,
The eldest son, Macdonnell's heir,
The foray's leader, when the clan
Fought with Mackenzies—man to man:
—Angus was tall and strong, they say,
As Coromandel's lithe Palmae,
And fearless as the stag whose leap
Is sure, or else—the death that's deep.

III.

The dews were light on Cillie-Christ,
And Janet Lyle's soft step the least
Of many gentle sounds that made
Her quick and venturous heart afraid:
But there was Angus coming near,
With smiles and words to calm her fear!
She loved the chief, Glengarry's son,
And he loved her—that love was one—
With graves whereon they stood that hour
Of omen, with the moonlit flower;
With all things deep and sad—with things
Whose timid promise never brings
The olive from the dove's wet wings.

IV.

Home from the foray's cheered success,
Macdonells turned, their band not less;
Mackenzies, in the Beauly firth,
Defeated, knew their valor's worth,
But swore with vengeance-bated breath,

To track young Angus to his death ,
Whose proud young steps did homeward turn—
They never came to Altsay burn !
The hill was steep, the foe's strong hand
Had signal tryst of all his band,
And cutting through the faithful ring,
That round a chief in clamor cling,—
With stubborn rage, deep wrath was hushed ;
With eyes that flamed, and cheek that flushed,
They closed and clenched in deadly grasp !
In silence, Angus—Donald's gasp
Was muttered, cursing, and—a minute,
Had all the fate of either in it !
Then Angus, with unplaided throat,
Turned faceward, saying, ere 'twas smote,
   "There, Donald Lyle, when I am slain,
   Tell *her* I would do this again ! "

v.

That day a lametation rose.
Glengarry's vales echoed their woes,
And rugged hearts, where grief was hard,
Pledged Clan Mackenzie sure reward.
Gather ! Gather ! from every hill,
Rang out, to Allen Mac Raonuill,—
The Lord of Lundy Leading them
Across the hills, whence late they came,
Well-favored, marching under night
On to the scene of speedy blight:
They reached it when the Sunday sun
With chapel service had begun ;

Then lighter grew each footstep's beat,
And whiter grew each cheek's white heat;
The distant twittering of a bird,
Could far on the birch-branch be heard—
The sacred walls of orison
Let no sight seen of anyone—
The sacred sound of prayer within
Made little note of outside din—
Till all surrounded it was held
At door and window sentineled:
And then—the very heart recoils,—
The red brands blaze around their spoils
To seething flames—the claymore's clash
Falls quickly, where the foremost's rash
In efforts to escape despair,
With cursing shriek or pleading pray'r,
The gasping breath, no more recalled—
All make the mind shrink back appalled;
And while the victims, tortured, die,
The Pibroch's shrill note heard on high,
With ghastly triumph made each death
A mockery in its mingled breath—
Of child and mother, man and man,
But few were left Mackenzie's clan.

VI.

But, in their turn, those few soon blent
To mustered strength with dire intent;
And, tracking dastard steps, took heed
Of twofold slaughter's double deed:
Dividing forces, two and two,

One, followed all the southside through,
Whose longest chase was over, when
Macdonnell's halted in the glen :
Then both the clans, though fainting, burned
With hot revenge, each deadly turned
Upon the other's rancorous wrath—
Their dead were mingled in their path—
Their mutual fury, strength of arm,
And swiftness kept an even charm :
At length Macdonnell's numbers, less,
Were driven in their last distress
To the wild torrent's rugged side—
In, tumbled, or were hurled, and died !

VII.

Mac Raonuill's strong, athletic frame,
Held longest to his valor's fame ;
And, having made his flight the best
To where the torrent tensely pressed—
A narrow chasm—death to miss—
He meant to leap the dread abyss :
While hot pursued, he took a glance—
The depth, the breadth, the desp'rate chance—
And blind with danger, fierce with hope,
With venture he would dare to cope :
Success ? Oh heavens ! his sure foot
Is safe !—Mackenzie in pursuit—
With less of strength and length of limb,
And less of the wild stag in him—
Leaps after, falling short—the brink
Grown sapling in his grasp must shrink !

" His life hangs clinging to its bough—
  What hope ? Shall malice spare him now ? "

Page 249.—Stanza VII.

His life hangs clinging to its bough—
What·hope? Shall malice spare him now?
Mac Raonuill turned—the dangling foe
Looked upward, in his eyes death's woe,
But on his proud lip not a word
Of suppliance, Mac Raonuill heard!
Mac Raonuill, coming nearer took
His dirk, with fiendish smile, and struck
The sapling, saying, "Take that too!
I've given much, to day, to you!"

TORTESA AND MURILLO.

A story is told of Murillo, which finely illustrates his power of truth and genius in sundering the bonds of adverse circumstances. Murillo had a mulatto slave, whom he employed in grinding his colors and performing the menial services of his studio. The students were sometimes annoyed at finding their work had been meddled with when they entered the studio in the morning; and as the touches, which their pictures received through the night, were superior to their own, they superstitiously believed that some supernatural agency was at work, and they charged the mulatto, who slept in the studio, to keep strict watch. This he promised to do; but what was their surprise, one morning, on observing a head of Venus, which their master had left upon his easel unfinshed, completely perfected, and in a style superior to anything Murillo had ever done. The master was astonished, and charged his pupils with meddling with his work. This they all positively denied; and poor Tortesa, the mulatto, was sternly commanded to tell all that had passed in the studio during his nightwatchings. At first, the terrified boy was silent; but at last he fell upon his knees, begged his master's pardon, and confessed that the work was his own. He had heard the instructions given to the pupils, and profited by them, unobserved. In a moment the countenance of Murillo was changed, and lifting up the astonished boy, he charged him to ask any favor, and it should be granted. Tortesa trembled, half doubting the sincerity of his master; but at last he found courage to say, "The liberty of my father." This was granted, but death early closed the career of him who gave such exalted evidence of genius. —*See Lossing's Fine Arts.*

TORTESA gronnd the colors for Murillo;
  Tortesa was a boy—a gold mulatto—
A genius, fervid as thy heart, O billow !
  A tryst with thy forever, O Tallatta !

The students wearing robes made note but lightly
   Of him—his menial service, dutiful:
Fair days were passing, and with sunsets brightly,
   Italian studios were beautiful.

For long the students wondered in the morning,
   What hand, with perfect touch their pictures made
Superior—some grace of new adorning,
   Put over, like a star, where ONE was laid.

They said unto each other, "something surely
   Worketh, in watchful night with perfect skill,
This mystery; for done most fair and purely,
   These lovely things beyond our own good will."

And then, one said: "Tortesa, here thou sleepest !
   Arise to-night, and watch, and hold thy peace,
And see who cometh when the hour is deepest !"
   Tortesa watched—the still stars of Venice,

He saw the master's work—a head of Venus,
   Not half complete, when left the night before:
His trust was deep, as sweet wells in Salinas,
   His heart struck, like a dipped gondola oar.

Murillo, seeing at the morn 'twas added
   To things made perfect, said: "I charge you all !
Which one will own to this ? " Then some evaded,
   And some denied, on some did silence fall.

Till, lo ! the silent slave, sternly commanded,
   Knelt down, confessing with a bended face:
"I heard thee, at closed doors, holding, faint handed,
   My heart, near where thy words had pleasant
     ways ! "

"Ah ! didst thou ?" said Murillo: "Ask some favor,
    While holding thee to heart, I love and hold !
Where utmost is my hope, thy least endeavor
    Falleth, like Indus waters, over gold ! "   ⌐

Tortesa, looking up, half doubting, trembled;
    But finding courage, said the words that live,
Long understood, where e'er, wherein dissembled :
    "My father's liberty, O Master, give ! "

SISTER MARY AGNES.

SISTER Mary Agnes, her cloister name--
    A nun, with large blue eyes, transparent hands :
She sat with us ; the white-clad windows' flame,
    Across the school-room floor, laid sunlight wands ;
And sometimes, when the noontide hour was still,
    And lull of lessons came, or humming task
Made more monotonous the effort's will,
    We wondered why she stopped—we dared not ask—
With shading hand she covered her blue eyes,
    Leaned slightly her veiled head ; to our replies
From reading classes, took no note,—did seem
    Abstracted, musing—did she pray or dream ?
I used to wonder, I, a little girl,
    That time, with cheek and brow shell-rose and pearl.

*   ❉   *   ❉   ❀

To-day is Springtide—many later years !
  Perhaps, like the caged bird, glad of release,
Long since to her, there came a death of Peace ;
  I think I see her folding in her sleeves,
Her delicate, fine hands enclasped and thin,
    And through her smiles there shown some light of
      tears,
And since, I've learned to tell the smile that grieves ;
  Remembering her glance as what hath been,
When with a soft foot stayed, she looked on me—
  Longest a little—ah ! what did she see ?
Perhaps, some prophecy her heart could tell,
  And one day she said something—all is well !
    ✿   ✿   ✿   ✿   ✿

Through all the long years, I remember her,
  A being of my childhood's mysteries—
A dweller in new lands—o'er traversed seas;
  To-day, the hills were blue—the heavens still;
A leaflet on the maples did not stir,
  I laid my hands across my face—what will
Of mine brought back to thought a shading hand ?
  I would not say I know, or understand—
I would not say, I saw it for a sign,
  So long since an unconscious Constantine !

A PHILOSOPHIC ASSURANCE.

A Druggist was sleeping quite soundly one night,
    When a rapping came loud at the door:
His wife, like the miller, awakened outright,
    As he suddenly stopped in a snore.

In no even temper, until his return,
    She lay still, and then grumbling, she said:
"Pray what did you sell, that its profits could earn
    Your arising just now from your bed ? "

"A hap'orth of salts ?   In good truth I should think
    That your profits are small on that dose,
For though sleep, to your eyes, may gradually wink,
    Yet an hour may elapse ere mine close ! "

"Be comforted, wife," the man amiably said ;
    "And well balanced content cultivate :
You're tangling just now your own destiny's thread,
    But view, also, this *other* man's state ! "

"While telling me now that my profits are small,
    Getting up, as you say, a point stronger—
But think, my dear wife, as you're thinking at all,
    That the *salts* will keep *him* up much longer ! "

THE "BEER SWILL."

Paris has her "Sans Culottes:" Naples her "Lazzaroni;" and San Francisco her "Beer Swills." The last cognomen is not so euphonious as the French or Italian, but it is not less significant of a special class. Though not so numerous as those of the European cities, we are not behind-hand in the quality of originality.

The "Beer Swill" proper, is only genuine in the neighborhood of "Tar Flat," although diversified specimens may be found in various other quarters. The particular individual who inspired the following lines, could be daily seen arising from just such a spot under the wooden sidewalk, and bearing his straw pallet to the adjacent lot, under the morning sun, while he meandered away to the nearest beer-kegs that were left outside the night before.

Occasionally, a comrade might be seen, arm in arm with him, in social chat; and together, their ragged elbows and unwashed faces might have eclipsed even Diogenes himself.

WARM glints of sun on soft acacia boughs,
The laugh of children down the sunny street,
The rustling flowret of the Autumn throws
Its last sweet beauty at the passer's feet :
It may be, he's a "keghouse vagrant," risen
From underneath the sidewalk where he lay;
That ragged thing there is his bed of hay—
Except occasionally when he's in prison—
He leaves it out to air it every day.

What distant ivy leaves, what sleepy stream,
What ring of happy voices now ne'er heard,
What fluttering bright wing of a captured bird,

Did stir last night in his uneasy dream?
Ah, sounding bells! afar, from distant shade,
Thy spell, a thought of childhood's home, hath made.

He's vacant looking with an ugly mug;
His sole possession is an empty can,
No doubt, at first it was a handsome jug,
But this is now to what his fortune ran:—
The bees still murmur in the distant hives,
And flower and stream are in the woody glade,
But, somehow, he has come on harder times,
A trembling wanderer and grown afraid;
He lets none see the silent tear that drops—
But keeps his eye upon the nearest "cops."